Backdated
DLA

STEPHEN GLENN LARGE

FOR ALL THE DLA FANS

I'd like to dedicate this book to all the DLA fans. Without your continued support I couldn't have afforded that fourth holiday this year.

CONTENTS

ACKNOWLEDGMENTS

To all the publishers who told me these kindle-topping books wouldn't sell.
Thanks.

1 CHRIS'MUS

Absolute bastard has 'made a wee start on Christmas'

A 35-year-old Belfast woman is getting on everyone's tits by boasting about how she's 'made a wee start on Christmas', it has emerged.

Smug Christine Kringle has been gloating to everyone around her about how organized she is this year.

The hairdresser bought most of her family's gifts online in July, therefore avoiding the Christmas price inflation and long queues at the shops.

Christine said, 'I'm totally organized this year, so I am. I've already got a load of people in. Means I can just relax and enjoy Christmas'.

In order to let everyone know how super-organized she is, Christine will begin every one of her conversations with the question, 'So, are ya all set for Christmas?'.

Once the unsuspecting person admits they haven't even started, Christine will proceed to tell them about all the toiletries and gift sets she wrapped up in July to get 'a wee head start'.

If this doesn't adequately panic the person, Christine will remind them how many shopping days and pay days it is until Christmas Eve.

However, her nephew Stuart has revealed that Christine's presents are 'usually shite'.

He said, 'It's the same aul keek every year. A Lynx Africa set and a three-pack of Primark trunks. No wonder the miserable bastard has her shopping finished in September'.

Belfast busker set to release Christmas album

A Romanian man dubbed 'the Transylvanian Tchaikovsky' is releasing a new album just in time for Christmas, according to reports.

Yohan Dracula (23) told his Twitter followers the tracks on the album will be covers of old Christmas classics using his trademark Stroh violin.

Over the past ten years, the busker has become as synonymous with Belfast City Centre as traffic congestion and unconscious junkies.

Yohan claims the instrument (made out of the horn from a gramophone and a broken violin) makes an even more annoying sound than Pete Snodden's voice.

His repetitive 'noise' can be heard bellowing from various doorways across the City until he is inevitably moved along by a rotund security guard with KFC gravy dripping down his navy blue jumper.

And now the busker is aiming for the Christmas #1 spot as he plans to release a Stroh inspired rendition of Paul McCartney's 'Wonderful Christmas Time'.

'He's definitely the most talented Romanian artist we've had in the UK since the Cheeky Girls were flashing their malnourished arses in glittery hotpants', claimed the editor of NME.

According to reports, pre-sales figures for the album, 'Stroh-Stroh-Stroh Merry Christmas' are particularly high in culturally-enriched Ballymena.

Complete arsehole puts her Christmas tree up

A Belfast woman has only gone and put her fucking Christmas tree up, it has emerged.

Christine Kringle from East Belfast made her husband (Nick) go up into the loft to fetch the tree before he went to work this morning.

The irritatingly cheerful woman then spent the morning turning her living room into 'some sort of fucking winter wonderland' according to Nick.

'It's not even Halloween yet for Christ's sake', moaned Nick.

'We'd both agreed after last year's fiasco that she'd wait until the start of December. But oh no, she was busting my balls about getting up into the loft for that tree as soon as I opened my eyes this morning', he added.

Then Christine nipped down to B&M Bargains to get herself some Christmas lights and a 'Santa, Please Stop Here' sign for the front garden.

Officials are concerned that the sight of Christine's tree through her living room window could spark a host of copycat tree-erections amongst neighbours who couldn't see green shite.

'That's it, I'll have my Albert up in the loft tonight', declared Christine's nosy bastard of a neighbour, Agnes.

Husband Nick was less than enthused about the situation.

'That'll be the house lit up like Blackpool illuminations for two full months. That reminds me, I may go and stick that magnet on the meter again'.

'That's it! I'm ringing Santa', threatens local mother

Desperate mothers across Northern Ireland are making bogus phone calls to an imaginary man in a bid to control their unruly brats, according to reports.

Throughout the year, naughty children are subjected to countless empty threats which have zero impact upon their awful behaviour.

But as Christmas fast approaches, mums are resorting to the ultimate scare tactic by threatening to phone Santa Claus himself.

Nikki Fibber, from Dundonald, struggled to control her three children this morning as she prepared to do the school run.

However, as soon she announced she was making a phone call to the North Pole, the little bastards became 'angels in disguise'.

She recalls, 'My four year old daughter was point blank refusing to take off her pyjamas'.

'So I whipped out my iPhone and I asked her, 'Do you want me to phone Santa?'. Within seconds she stripping like Gypsy Rosie Lee'.

'If I'd known it was so effective, I'd have started threatening them with this in the summer'.

Tanya Teller from Tullycarnet told us when her own children misbehave, she cups her hands around her mouth and shouts at the sky 'Santa, do you see this?'.

'They completely shite themselves and immediately stop what they're doing', she cackled.

'Sometimes I mix it up and tell them they're going to wake up on Christmas morning to a beg of ashes'.

'We've an electric fire, so I'm not sure they even know what a beg of ashes is but it shuts the wee fuckers up anyway'.

Sally Squib keeps her offspring under control by constantly reminding them that 'Santa's watchin ya know?'.

She explained, 'I was trying to watch Jezza Kyle in peace when the twins kept asking for a drink of juice. So I told them, 'Santa's watching ya know' and they left me alone until the ad break'.

Her son, Ben (3), is becoming increasingly concerned about the number of entities watching his every move.

He told us: 'It's not bad enough I've got Jesus and God watching me 24hrs a day, now Santa too?

'Have these fuckers nothing better to do with their time? No wonder the world's ravaged by war and famine if God spends his entire day watching whether or not I finish my dinner or put my toys away'.

Local man Spanker Thompson recalls his parents using the same threats when he was a young child.

'It wasn't just Santa I got threatened with. It was numerous other imaginary entities such as the Easter Bunny and the Tooth Fairy as well. Thank God I don't believe in those anymore', he said.

Facebook announces new 'the boy done good' filter for Christmas

Social media giants Facebook will offer its users a new filter allowing them to block any 'the boy did good' posts from their timelines on Christmas Day this year, according to reports.

Every Christmas, thousands of women pretend to be shocked while posing for photographs with all the gifts they demanded from their partners before posting them on social media.

Images of the gifts, packaging and in some cases, receipts, are cropped, filtered and then sent into cyberspace with the sole intent of turning others green with envy.

CEO Mark Zuckerberg told us:

'Now that Facebook is nearly 15 years old and we absolutely despise everyone on our 'friends' list, we thought we'd make things a more tolerable by censoring what most of the bragging fuckers got for Christmas'.

'The boy done good' Facebook posts have become as synonymous with the modern Christmas as Schloer and people moaning about the ever decreasing size of Quality Street tins.

And failure to adhere to these materialistic demands will often result in the end of the relationship between the female and her beleaguered companion.

Wee Nick Noel (27) from Belfast, recalls how his four-year relationship ended last Christmas when he failed to deliver a Jo Malone candle that his girlfriend had demanded.

He told us, 'I spent months gathering together all the items on the list she gave me. I just forgot that fucking candle'.

'She went ballistic. It didn't matter about all the other stuff I did remember'.

'She didn't even write 'the boy did alright' or anything. I just got dumped'.

Meanwhile, DFS have reported a 76% increase in long sofa sales as mothers compete to see who has bought their kids the most unnecessary expensive gifts this year.

Big Sandra from The Braniel told us:

'It's all-out war this year. I had to order a bigger sofa cos I got our Riley a Mac Book Pro'.

'You get a 3-year warranty with it which is handy because he's only 6-months old and accidents will happen like'.

36-year-old man getting socks and Lynx sets for Christmas

A Dundonald man is set to receive socks and Lynx sets for the fourth consecutive Christmas, it has emerged.

After waking up on Christmas morning the past three years to find only novelty socks and a Lynx Body Spray and Wash Duo Gift Set under the tree, Chrissy Kringle (36) has resigned himself to idea that this year will be no different.

The uninspiring gifts have led Chrissy to ponder whether or not he'll even bother getting out of bed at all this year.

'I might just lie on', explained Chrissy

'A fucking 3-pack of Star Wars socks out of Primark and a £2.49 Lynx Africa set. Hardly worth getting out of bed for'.

These disappointing experiences have left the 36-year-old with a rather grim outlook regards the festive season.

'Christmas? The same aul shite every year, so it is'.

'Sitting in a living room watching Home Alone for the 400th time with all the people you try to avoid the other 364 days a year'.

'Everyone wearing ridiculous jumpers and throwin' Quality Street down their fat necks while a Brussel sprout fart-cloud hangs in the atmosphere like a layer of smog'.

'Christmas mornings used to be about Xboxes and Blu-Rays. But as soon as you hit your 30s, people just stop putting the effort in'.

'Lazy, unimaginative bastards the lot of them'.

When asked what he got his wife and kids for Christmas, Chrissy replied 'Amazon vouchers'.

Dundonald 'Contimental' market comes to town

The Dundonald 'Conti-mental' market opened to a record crowd of five people last night.

Every year, people who like to try 'something a wee bit different' visit the market, which comes to town in exactly the same format as the year before.

The market, consisting of two stalls, is situated on Church Road where the old butchers used to be, before he was shut down for flushing pig's heads down the shitter.

Locals are invited to come along and sample the exotic cuisine from faraway places like Ards, Comber and Sydenham.

Customers can treat their palates to such delicacies as cheese & pickled onion on cocktail sticks, frankfurters from a tin or 'tamata & spam samiches'.

Then they are invited to wash it down with a diverse range of alcoholic beverages such as Tennents, Carlsberg and Harp.

But it's not all about Dad guzzling cheap lager or Mum gobbling big German sausages. Kids are also encouraged to come along to see Dundonald's Santa Claus, now that he's allowed to work with children again.

Market organiser Giorgi Venal told assembled press about some new features in this year's market.

He said, 'We've got a completely different layout this year. We put the beer stall on the left and the spam wagon on the right'.

First customer of the night, wee Sadie from Dunlady Park said, 'I love the cuntimental market, so a do. Just gets ye in the Chris'mas spurit, doesn't it?'

'Me and our Albert come down an get a tin of Harp and hat-dawg and just soak up the atmosphere. There's naffin like a bitta warm meat inside ye on a cowl night', she added.

Flight attendant Simon Brown from Ballyreagan Road beamed, 'Oh mummy, I just love the market. Looking forward to hitting it later on. I haven't had a bitta German sausage since my last stop over in Hamburg'.

However, Sally Highbrow from neighbouring Hillsborough was less complimentary about her experience.

'The place was crawling with the dregs of society. I noticed some peasant woman was wearing hideous sheepskin boots. I think they were called Uggs or something ghastly like that', said Sally.

'Then I asked the vendor if I could have a crepe and he told me 'If you're gonna take a shite luv, do it round the back where the kids won't see ye'. I was absolutely mortified', she added.

'Just get me anything for Christmas' says world's fussiest fucker

A local woman is adhering to her annual strategy of being absolutely no help when It comes to choosing her Christmas gift, according to reports.

Every year without fail, Miriam McMelter (44) refuses to be drawn into specifics by her husband, Herbie, when he quizzes her about a suitable Yuletide prezzie.

Despite weeks of prodding her on the subject, Miriam usually fobs him off with a statement like, 'Ach just get me anything'.

However, whenever Herbie reluctantly uses his initiative and selects a gift he thinks she'd love and appreciate, he discovers on Christmas morning he was totally wrong.

'Just get me anything she says', sighed Herbie whilst having a crafty fag in his garden shed.

'No matter what I pick, her face always hurts her on Christmas morning', he revealed.

'She doesn't even attempt to mask her disappointment when she opens the gift. Not even a thank you. First thing she asks is, 'Do you still have the receipt?'. I think I'd prefer it if she just said it was shite. It'd be less hurtful', he sobbed.

Miriam gave us an insight into what happened last Christmas in her own words. She said, 'When has he ever seen me wearing a fuckin' cardigan – in his life??'.

'What am I? 60 or somethin'?, she quizzed.

'I must be the easiest person in the world to buy for, sure I have nothin'?'.

'Anything, anything at all. But he better not just hand me money this year and tell me to get myself something in the sales. The lazy useless fucker', she added.

'I'll probably just give her money this year. Let her get herself something in the sales', said Herbie all pleased with himself.

Michaella McCollum to switch on Dundonald's Christmas lights

Local importer/ exporter Michaella McCollum has been invited to turn on Dundonald's Christmas lights, it has been revealed.

The former dancer has been keeping a low profile since she was released from prison but it would appear that Lisburn and Castlereagh Borough Council have managed to secure her first PA gig.

The switch on of the assorted bulbs is one of the biggest occasions in the local calendar.

Every year, dozens of people not shackled by the commitment of employment brave the wintery conditions to see a Z-List Celeb turn on the lights.

Securing McCollum is seen as a bit of a coup for the Super-Council after last year's underwhelming appointment of Jamie Dornan's cousin's uncle's sister's brother-in-law.

A copy of McCollum's rider has been leaked to a local paper, in which, the Dungannon woman demanded a 3kg bag of Quaker Oats, a variety of hair scrunchies and a German Shepherd with no sense of smell.

Local primary school children dressed as shepherds will badly sing a few hymns for the gloomy damp crowd.

Choir boy Harry Spence, 6, told us, 'I hope my ma makes an effort this time round. Four full weeks she had to get her shit together last year and I got sent to school with a tea towel strapped to my head'.

Meanwhile, ultra-competitive father Paul Smyth is just delighted that his two-month-old son has been selected to play baby Jesus.

He told us, 'We put Paul Jnr through a rigorous regime to get him prepared for the role. He's been sleeping in a barn up at Streamvale Farm for the last three weeks'.

'I know it's a bit nippy but we thought if we were going to do this then we were going to do it properly. So he's been sleeping in a wicker basket wearing nothing but a shapeless woven tunic'.

Michaella said, 'It's gonna be a white Christmas alright'.

Elf on the Shelf fed up with lazy parent's half-hearted attempts

Everybody's favourite little Elf has confessed that he would like to be put back up in the loft, it has emerged.

Despite being only five days into his annual month long Facebook tour, the Elf, real name Wayne Hamilton, claims he's had enough of parent's half-hearted attempts this year.

'I woke up in the cupboard under the stairs this morning, again', revealed Wayne.

'It's only the 5th December and those lazy bastards have forgotten to put me in a mischievous and hilarious pose two nights out of four. It's insulting', he barked.

However, Frank Stewart (39), shifted full responsibility for the Elf duties onto his wife, Angie (35), this year.

'I'm sick of the sight of that creepy-looking, pointy-hatted, rosy-cheeked little fucker', moaned Frank.

"Oh, look how creative and imaginative we are". It's just another Facebook cock-measuring contest, like Halloween'.

'Ten times last year we'd just got into bed, next thing she's jumping out of it and away down the stairs cos she's forgotten to do the Elf'.

'Never mind Elf on a Shelf. What about a ride with my bride?', questioned Frank.

Wife Angie is already ruing the decision to bring the Elf down from the roof space. She said, 'Maybe Frank was right. Trying to come up with fresh ideas every night is a right pain in the ovaries'.

'I might just give the kids some bullshit excuse about not wanting them to think they're under surveillance or that they shouldn't focus their lives around materialistic goals. Either that or just tell them the Elf, Santa and Christmas is all one big fucking lie'.

But Wayne the Elf has a cunning plan to get even with the perfunctory pathetic parents.

'Maybe I should start reporting back to Santa what Frank and Angie are up to instead? Frank's Pornhub usage is up 20% on last year and Angie's necking a glass of wine before the school run. Then we'll see who's on the fucking naughty list?'.

Local man finally runs out of last year's toiletries

Dundonald man Davy Gabbana has revealed that he's used up the toiletries he was bought at Christmas 2017, two weeks shy of this year's festive holiday.

The part-time joiner - who is also a 'full-time mad bastard' according to his Facebook account - only managed to spray his left armpit in Lynx Chocolate this morning before the aerosol ran done.

The 28-year-old discovered that his V05 texturising hair product had also been used and resorted to using his wife's hairspray which he inadvertently blinded himself with before leaving the house.

He told us, 'I'm just hoping to get through the next fourteen days until this year's batch of toiletries arrives'.

'At first, I started to get a bit of a complex because everyone kept buying me aftershaves and deodorants for Christmas. But then I realised that once you hit a certain age, no one has a fuckin' clue what to buy ye, so a wee Lynx set is always a safe bet'.

He added, 'From about January to June you're strutting around like something outta GQ magazine. From July to October you start to ration your smellies and by November you're using the wife's hair mousse and Impulse body Spray'.

His mate, wee Ricky Rabanne, was the butt of many jokes in work this morning after an unfortunate incident involving his wife's tanning moisturiser.

The 32-year-old ran out of his usual post-shave ointment and decided to use his wife's gradual self-tanning lotion.

Unfortunately the carpet-fitter applied too much of the product to his face and by tea-break time the results were evident.

He said, 'The boys were rippin' the back clean outta me. I'd fuckin' dyed my eyebrows the heap. My bake was so orange the parades commission tried to stop me driving to work this morning'.

'Put that back in the fridge - it's for Christmas' says local woman

Mothers across Dundonald are dishing out repeated bollockings over their family's attempts to eat foods reserved for Jesus' birthday bash.

With fridges at full capacity and resembling some sort of edible game of Tetris, crafty children and husbands across BT16 keep sneaking a peak at the delicious bounty only to be told - 'put it back, it's for Chris'muss'.

Big Janice from Coronation Park put her husband of 13 years in hospital over an After Eight he tried to pinch.

Speaking from the specialist trauma ward of the Ulster Hospital, her husband Roy told us, 'I was lookin' for somethin' to have with a wee cuppa tea and ya never see those delicious wafer thin chocolate mints in the house apart from Christmas'.

'There's about 90 of them in a bax but that aul bat still brained me with a rollin' pin before shoutin', 'they're for Christmas'.

Little Noel, 6, was threatened with an 'aul beg of ashes' unless he stopped asking for a glass of Shloer.

He told us, 'It's the same story every year. We're all eating fish finger sandwiches for a week whilst the fridge is filled with a banquet fit for a king'.

'Then on Christmas Day, the food that's thrown out could nourish a small African tribe for a month. Then we hear the old war cry 'I'm nat buyin as much next year, luk at the waste, lat's a sin' - only for the silly bitch to buy the same amount if not more the following Christmas'.

'And why did she buy a 3kg bag of sprouts when she's the only one who eats them? Did Jesus even eat sprouts? Why am I forced to eat them if beardy didn't even like them?', he questioned.

Big Janice defended herself by saying, 'You'd swear some of them had never seen food before. That fridge door's been opened more times than Taylor Swift's legs. I've had to put a fuckin energy saving light bulb in it'.

'Then on Chris'muss Day and there's a terrible amount of waste. So, I just tell them, 'think a lem poor Biafran childer'.

'I don't know why I say that to be fair? Tellin' someone who's already full up to gorge on more food while thinking of a starving African is a bit sick in the head', she added.

Local man sues Mariah Carey over misleading lyrics

A man from Morven Park in Ballybeen Estate is taking legal action against Grammy winning artist Mariah Carey over what he claims are 'misleading lyrics' in her Christmas hit 'All I Want For Christmas Is You'.

Stanley Skinflint, 35, heard his long-term girlfriend belting out the words to Mariah Carey's 1994 Christmas hit whilst they were driving to do some last minute Christmas shopping.

It was whilst listening to the lyrics of the song that his girlfriend was singing with such conviction that Stanley had an epiphany.

He explains, 'We were on our way down to Connswater Shappin' Centre and were stuck in traffic in Ballyhack'.

'As soon as that 'All I Want For Christmas Is You' came on the radio the missus burst into song. I still hadn't got her any presents and was starting to panic'.

'But when it came to the chorus and she started pointing at me while singing 'All I want for Christmas is you', I firmly believed she did not care about the materialistic trappings and gifts associated with Christmas, and all she wanted was to spend it with me'.

'So I nipped into the card shap and bought a huge red ribbon. On Christmas morning when she came down the stairs, sprawled across the sofa where her presents would usually be, was me ballick naked with the big bow on my head'.

'At first she laughed hysterically. But once she realised I'd bought her fuck all, she went mental and started throwing decorations at me. I ended up standing on a bauble and cut the fut clean aff myself'.

'She threw me out on Christmas day and I didn't get back into the house until I'd spunked about two grand on a credit card in the January sales. Then she was able to stick a photo of her Michael Korrs watch on facebook and say 'le boy done good'.

Mr Skinflint is now suing Mariah Carey for supplying misleading information, emotional distress and the price of a Michael Korrs watch.

Local man recovering well after dressing gown amputation

A Belfast man is said to be in a stable condition after undergoing an operation to have his dressing gown removed.

The 35-year-old is recovering well in the Specialist House Coat Unit of the Ulster Hospital after the complicated five hour procedure.

Nick Noel was admitted to hospital last night after his dressing gown became fused to his flesh. The garment attached itself to Mr Noel's body due to the length of time he'd spent inside it over the Christmas holidays.

Speaking from his hospital bed, Mr Noel told us, 'The surgeon told me there'd be some permanent scarring but he managed to remove around 95% of my house coat'.

'I just lost track of time. I was sat on the sofa watching Dad's Army drinking Bucks Fizz for what must've been weeks'.

Another man was also admitted to hospital last night when he overdosed on stuffing. Jeremy Paxo, 45, was found face down on the floor in a pile of breadcrumbs and sausage meat by his wife.

She told us, 'the greedy ballix had his head in that fridge every five minutes. The doctor said his heartburn had heartburn'.

In other news, the Department of Pointless Statistics have revealed that 87% of people still off work think that every day is a Sunday.

Man cries during post-Christmas commute

A grown man burst into floods of tears this morning in his car whilst stuck in traffic.

Stevie McGreedy was returning to work after two weeks off when he suddenly lost control of his emotions.

'It's so bloody dark, it's just not natural', he sobbed.

McGreedy spent the better part of the past fortnight functioning to the lowest possible level, draped in a new dressing gown.

He was just growing accustomed to his new lifestyle when suddenly, he was thrust back into his old routine of 6am starts and monotonous employment.

He explained, 'I felt a lump in my throat as soon as the alarm went off. Thankfully the rest of my family were still sleeping because had anyone engaged me I may have broken down in front of them'.

'Once I stepped outside into the pissing rain and got inside my car, I was an emotional wreck. I knew tears were imminent', he continued,

He explained, 'In hindsight, it really wasn't the brightest idea to spend a fortnight developing a reverse sleeping pattern. I mean, sitting up to 3am every night watching shite films was probably the worst decision since Gary Glitter decided to get his PC repaired'.

He also developed a mild case of agoraphobia over the course of his holiday. He told us, 'with the exception of the odd trip to put something out in the bin, I managed to avoid leaving the house. The place was filled with a variety of cooked meats and alcohol, there was no real necessity to leave'.

He added, 'but after spending a fortnight using my colon as beer slide for chocolate and stuffing, I've rendered my immune system worse than a member of the Dallas Buyers Club'.

Man seeking plausible Dry January exit strategy

A Dundonald man is actively searching for a credible excuse to end his miserable self-imposed drink embargo, it has emerged.

Stephen McGreedy, 36, decided to give up the booze for a month after friends and family subtly pointed out that 'he'd completely ripped the hole out of it' over the festive period.

However, nine days into sobriety, McGreedy has begun to question not only his decision but the very essence of his own existence.

'Oh fuck this', sobbed McGreedy. 'I can't do this for another three weeks. There has to be a way out of it?'.

After scrolling through his Facebook account, the 36-year-old made a startling discovery.

'I was hoping there'd be some unavoidable social event that would be swimming in glorious booze but there's nothing. No stag dos, no weddings – not even a birthday. Not one fucker I know was born in January, what are the odds, eh?'

'All I can pray for now is a death. Funerals are generally monumental piss ups. I'll ring my ma and see how my aunt Ethel's getting on. Heard they spotted something in her lung in November. She could be my ticket to an early bevvy'.

McGreedy's voluntary exile from alcoholism had led him to make, with a little encouragement from his spouse, some bold and semi-permanent life choices.

'She made me join the gym with her', said McGreedy whilst sat on the sofa in his expensive new tracksuit eating a Pot Noodle.

'The PT said I'll be using a few machines tonight. Hopefully it's the gamblies in the fuckin' bar', he added.

January enters third month

As January enters its third month so far, millions of people across the globe are wondering if it will ever fucking end.

With no end in sight, experts have warned it could last as long as FIVE YEARS.

'We all know January's a bit of a bastard to get through but this year it's just taking the piss', said Prof. Duncan D. Nutt of Dundonald Tech.

'It feels like we're living in dog years. I think next year we should agree to skip the fucker all together and go straight into February. A nice wee 28-day jobby'.

It's been a particularly gruelling experience for those who stupidly volunteered to abstain from alcohol and many are at their wits end.

'Every morning I wake up praying it's February', confessed Stephen McGreedy.

'If ever there was a month you need to drink yourself into oblivion it's this one'.

'The weather's shite, the kids are sick so can't leave the house and I've ate my body weight in Terry's Chocolate Orange segments'.

'You know you've put the beef on when the wife tells you to come on your own tits', he moaned.

Orange Order to release new series of L.O.L. Dolls for Xmas

The Orange Order is launching its own version of a popular children's toy in an attempt to attract younger female members into its ranks, according to reports.

LOL Surprise Dolls are the new toy phenomenon that have swept the world.

Now the Loyal Orange Institution is hoping to capitalize on this by developing its own staunchly Protestant play-things.

So what are LOL dolls? Basically, they are small dolls wrapped in a surprise egg. Like Kinder Eggs only a lot more expensive.

If you've a daughter under the age of ten, chances are you've been subjected to countless 'unboxing' videos on YouTube.

These normally involve a creepy middle-aged woman talking incessant shite while unwrapping dozens of toys.

The new Loyal Orange Lodge dolls will be hitting the shelves just in time for Christmas and are expected to be No.1 on all Loyalist children's lists to Santa.

There are 45 Loyal Orange Lodge dolls to collect including Purple Star Queen and Kozy Club Babe.

Each collectible comes with a host of 'Prod' accessories including a band stick, a flute, an accordion and even a ceremonial sword.

'It will be this year's most sought after toy in the PUL community', beamed Grand Master Craig James while unboxing a selection of Loyal Orange Lodge dolls at a press conference.

'Weaker! An ultra-rare', he screamed while holding his glittery miniature aloft.

2 DUNDANAL

**'That ball comes in my garden again, I'll stick a knife in it',
shouts old bastard.**

An angry old bastard has threatened to burst a child's football using a
knife should it ever find its way into her garden again, it has emerged.

Ethel McGulder (86) was looking out her window hoping to be
offended by something when as luck would have it, an all-weather size 4
Mitre soccer ball landed in her meticulously kept garden.

When an 8-year-old boy came into the garden to fetch it, the retired
teacher appeared at her front door and yelled, 'If that ball comes in my
garden again, I'll stick a knife in it'.

When the frightened little boy ran off, Ethel lifted the ball and placed it
inside her shed alongside the countless others she's confiscated over the
years.

Throughout the 70s, 80s and 90s, Ethel chastised hundreds of children
that had strayed into her garden in search balls, Frisbees and other
misplaced items.

But the past fifteen years or so have proved to be a barren spell for
grumpy old fuckers like Ethel.

The emergence of electrical devices such as iPads, smartphones and tablets has resulted in a sharp decline in the amount of feral children meandering the streets looking for adults to antagonise or things to set-alight.

'Ah, it was just like the aul days', smiled Ethel.

'About twen'y years ago, you'd hardly gat yer arse back to yer seat and some other wee fucker's ball wudda landed in yer garden'.

Justifying her behaviour, including threatening a small child with a blade, Ethel reasoned:

'There's a big field over there, if they wanna kick futbal. What if they put someone's windies in? Who's gonna pay fer that?'

'Besides, me and my Albert can hardly hear the TV over it', she said, whilst turning the volume up to 99 bars.

Dundonald's oldest man dies, 42

A self-employed tiler who was thought to be Dundonald's oldest man and put his longevity down to drinking ethanol has died, aged 42.

James Thompson, also known locally as Jim, Jimmy and Jamesy, died on Tuesday evening just 16 days before his 43rd birthday.

Jim was tragically killed when his eyebrows caught fire whilst trying to light a joint off a toaster.

Last October he was named the oldest man in Dundonald according to the website 'Oldest in Britain'.

People who knew Jim put his extraordinarily long existence down to his diet and active lifestyle.

'He must've been a fitness fanatic. He was always wearing tracksuits', said his neighbour Sally Tattler.

'Most parents round here would send their kids to school in a taxi'

'But I saw Jim walking the full 300 yards to the school gate with his child some mornings', she added.

Jim's diet was believed to be exemplary by local standards.

'He always asked for boiled rice with his salted-chilli chicken and now & again took salad on his kebab' remarked Big Iris McDowell, owner of Jim's local take-away.

Some people were worried that Jim wouldn't even see 25 at one point given his youthful penchant for glue-sniffing and 10% proof Scandinavian beers.

'Jim really defied the ageing process by cutting back on the drink. By the time he was 32 he was drinking as little as 14 cans a night. I don't know where he got his willpower from?' said his younger brother Mark.

Moat Park bridge reapplies for drinking licence

The old foot bridge in the moat park looks set to reapply for its drinking license after an online petition was started by concerned local residents, according to reports.

The bridge was once a thriving night spot where local teens would drink to excess before vomiting where they stood.

Big Davy Weir, 47, from Morven Park is concerned that his 15-year-old son is missing out on some of the greatest nights of his life because drinking alcohol in the Moat Park has been banned by Lisburn & Castlereagh Council.

He said, 'I'm growin' increasingly concerned about our Jordan. His jeans are so friggin' tight they luk like they've been vacuum formed around his legs'.

'He spends his Friday nights in his room poutin like a duck, takin selfies and stickin lem online'.

'I 'member when I was his age a Friday night involved sitting at the bridge and tankin' 5 tins of Royal Dutch and a battle'a Old E'.

'Then we'd meet up with la rest a la skinheads and knock seventeen shades of shite out of each other. Lose wore la days'.

Neil Stewart, 35, who spent the better of the 90s sitting on the wall, complained:

'It's an absolute disgrace that the bridge is being used solely as a pedestrian overpass lccse days.

'Kids are missin out big time. I member we used to bring an aul beat-bax down 'n listen til a bitta Danny Dee while palishin aff a crate of Orange WKD'.

'If ya were lucky ya went home with yer finger nails smellin like you'd munched a multi-pack a Scampi Fries'.

Gregg Martin spent every night Friday at the Moat Bridge until its closure around ten years ago.

He suggested, 'Drinking at the Moat Bridge should be made compulsory. Kids these days are too busy trying to get into university but life's real education happened here at the bridge'.

'Do ya know many 14-year-olds nowadays that cud hold two battered sausages with one hawnd and fair dig someone from Tullycarnet with the other? No way ya wud'.

Translink to bring back the No8 service

Translink have announced that they're bringing back the No.8 Ballybeen Estate bus due to overwhelming public demand.

The move comes after community representatives stormed Translink HQ and 'had a wee word' with bosses about restoring the much cherished service.

'We can confirm that the No.8 bus will return to active service, just as soon as we find someone mental enough to drive it', said a Translink spokesperson.

The news was greeted with cheers as a crowd of locals had gathered outside Translink's Head Office on East Bridge Street.

'Ach we're over the moon so we are', beamed 82-yr-old Ethel Tattler from Drumadoon Drive.

'Thon Glider was a full ballix. What would an aul doll like me need Hi-Fi for anyways? Sure I don't even have a FaceTube account'.

'To be honest, I'm looking forward to having a wee feg on the buses again'.

'It must be 25 years since I've sparked a Superking Menthol while sat beside a young mother and her 3-year-old chile', recalled Ethel.

Local man 'Dopey' Dave McBride is looking forward to showing his teenage son how to hitch a ride by stowing away inside the bus's boot.

'Our Nathan's never experienced the joy of running down Culross Drive after the No.8 and sneaking a lift down the road inside its boot'.

'That's how I got this', said Dave whilst pointing at a nine inch scar running down the left-hand-side of his face.

Meanwhile 77-year-old Cecil Greener cannot wait to clear the phlegm in his chest by spitting it all over the floor at the back of the bus.

'That's why kids these days are constantly sick. They're not exposed to enough germs', spluttered Cecil while gobbing a lump of mucus onto the backboard of the seat in front.

Following the news, there have also been calls to reinstate the No.188 school bus which used to depart from the old Ballybeen Square.

Retired driver Alex Dennis, 64, had the enviable duty of transporting a carriage full of unruly spotty little bastards to Grosvenor High School every morning for the better part of a decade.

When Mr Dennis was informed about the news at his home in Gilnahirk, a tear of pride fell from his eye that wasn't permanently damaged by laser pens.

The retired bus driver then recounted some of the harrowing journeys he made through the suburbs of East Belfast two decades ago.

He said, 'I remember the day I was told I'd be driving the 188 bus. My hands trembled as I looked at that route which started in Ballybeen Square'.

He continued, 'I then had to navigate my way past Tullycarnet and then onto the Braniel. It was almost as if someone hand-picked the most mental places in East Belfast for a laugh'.

'Stop after stop, hordes of these acne-riddled boys with curtain haircuts got on. They were putting all sorts of body fluids onto crumpled up pages and throwing them at each other'.

'A combination of bad breath and body heat meant that the windows were steamed up to the point I was literally driving blind through housing estates'.

'Being stabbed in neck with a compass or struck full force in the temple with a rubber was pretty distracting too'.

'Occasionally, someone would draw a large spunking penis on the window. I could just about see through the outline and managed to get to the Castlereagh Road where I'd unload the fuckers'.

Despite the horrible experiences, Alex considers himself one of the lucky ones. He told us, 'At least I got the morning shift when most of them were still half asleep or hungover. My mate Dessie got the 3.20pm slot. He couldn't live with what he'd witnessed and threw himself under his own bus four years ago'.

Dundonald couple set to divorce after building flat-pack wall unit

A Dundonald couple are divorcing after six years of marriage following a failed attempt to build flat-pack furniture from IKEA, it has emerged.

Helen and Joe McMelter made the decision about four hours into their futile bid to assemble a 'Liatorp' wall unit during which the frailties of their relationship were brutally exposed.

Despite the protestations of a mildly hungover Joe, Helen insisted upon visiting the notorious Swedish hell-hole where she spotted the 9ft wide and 7ft high unit.

It wasn't until they arrived home and started unpacking the various boxes that the enormity of the task at hand became apparent.

And several hours of swearing and finger pointing, the unit, much like their marriage, came crashing down around them.

At one point the PSNI were called to property by a concerned neighbour who heard 'a womanly cry for help'.

However, when officers arrived on the scene they found Joe lying in the corner of the living room with a 32-page instruction manual lodged up his rectum.

After the police had diffused the situation, the couple decided it was best to dissolve the marriage immediately and left the matter in the hand of their respective legal teams.

Dr Steph O'Scope of Dundonald Looniversity believes that a trip to IKEA followed by a collaborative effort to build flat-pack furniture is the true test of any relationship.

'When you're two hours into building an IKEA unit, that's when you see someone's true colours'.

'If at the end of it all you've a fully-built unit with zero spare parts and you haven't stuck an allen key up your spouse's hole, then it's time to start booking that Platinum Wedding Anniversary party', she added.

'I told the useless bastard to use the instructions. But no. He knew better', recalled Helen.

'IKEA must be the Swedish word for divorce', said Joe.

North Korean rocket hits Ballybeen

A housing estate on the outskirts of East Belfast was rocked to the core this morning when it was hit by a stray North Korean missile.

The long-range missile exploded on a patch of grass facing Davaar Avenue causing damage to the surrounding properties, although miraculously, no one was injured.

An announcement on North Korea state television said a Hwasong-14 missile was tested on Tuesday, overseen by leader Kim Jong-un who had just defeated a brick wall in a game of tennis in straight sets.

Unfortunately, a highly-intoxicated Kim Jong-un entered the wrong coordinates and the intercontinental ballistic missile (ICBM) landed in Ballybeen.

'Ballistic missile? Wait til my ma sees her washing. Then you'll see f**kin' ballistic mate. There's mud all over her whites', raged local woman Tracey-Ann.

'There are enough rockets around here love, we don't need any Korean ones', added Ginny, 71, who came out 'for a wee nosy' after the missile exploded.

Shortly after the explosion, a statement was released by the estate's own ballistics squad.

'The Ballybeen Rocket Team is on standby. We'll be sending a few incontinent rockets in your man Kim Jong-un's direction as soon as one of the lads gets back with an atlas'.

'I hear the capital of North Korea is Pyongyang. That's the same noise this frying pan will make when I whack Kim Jong-un around the bake with it', they added.

One in four Dundonald children still forced to carry PE kits in plastic bag from off licence

The latest figures from the NSPCC reveal that one in four Dundonald children are still forced to carry their PE kits to school in a plastic bag from a local off licence.

For decades, binge-drinking parents have saved a fortune on expensive PE equipment for their children by stashing all their carry-out bags in a kitchen drawer usually reserved for pointless shite such as batteries, odds and playing cards.

Big Ethel from Ballybeen Estate packs her son's sportswear in the same bags she uses to transport her Vat 19 home from Winemark on a Friday night.

'Our Jamie's to go swimming the mara, so I'll stick a wee pair-a-trunks inside a Winemark beg for him', she explained.

'But he better bring it back home the wee ballix- his da needs that beg for his piece as well'.

The tradition is reportedly encouraged by gossiping teachers who are then able to decipher which children's parents are the piss-poor heavy drinkers, without having to ask anyone directly.

P7 teacher Mrs Busybody told us:

'The staff room is always a hive of activity as we try to establish whose parents are the most impoverished'.

'Plastic bags and non-uniform days are a great way of spotting which ones are the scummy tramps'.

Ethel's son, Jamie, is less enthused about the situation.

'When we go swimming, I always get changed beside big dopey Robert'.

'He's so hairy and well-hung he looks like Ron Jeremy with hypertrichosis and I'm stood next to him looking like I've embarked upon a course of electrolysis'.

He continued, 'So, as if that wasn't bad enough, now I'm being sent to school with my swimming trunks in a plastic bag. She couldn't embarrass me enough.'.

'Big Ethel's been humiliating me for years. Everyone else in my class is running about in fancy Gola sneakers and drinking Pepsi-Max, and here's me wearing a pair of King Fishers and swigging diluted juice from an aul Smack Cola bottle'.

Meanwhile, Jamie's classmate 'Crazy' Andy doesn't see what all the fuss is about:

'Dunno what the fuck he's moaning about. What I'd give for a plastic beg. My ma just sent me out the door with my trunks wrapped in a towel'.

Man miraculously avoids entering McDonalds Drive-Thru

A Dundonald man managed to drive past McDonalds without succumbing to temptation and entering the Drive-Thru, it has emerged.

Unbelievably 37-yr-old Phil O'Fish was able to steer his vehicle past the fast food joint in a straight line and did not end up with a greasy brown paper bag bulging with delicious salted bounty on his passenger seat.

It's the first time since the franchise opened in 1992 that anyone has been able to resist the overwhelming urge to swing their car into the Drive-Thru.

'Don't ask me how I did it', implored Phil.

'Usually when I see those golden arches and the smell of cooked reconstructed meat engulfs the car, without thinking I'll swing the car into that bloody Drive-Thru'.

'And before you know it, you're at the speaker ordering a Big Mac Meal, six nuggets and some of those cheese bites'.

'It doesn't matter how big a bloody dinner you had either. There's always room for a McDonalds'.

'But tonight, I dunno what came over me. I just kept the blinkers on and put my foot down', he explained.

However, Phil's neighbour Mick Flurry was not so lucky.

Despite having a hefty Chinese take-away for his tea, the 29-year-old succumbed to temptation when picking his wife up after she finished her 10pm shift at work.

'I wasn't even fucking hungry', recalled Mick.

'The missus hadn't had any dinner and asked me to swing into the Drive-Thru'.

'After I'd placed her order the guy on the headset asked me 'Is that all?'. I just crumbled'.

'I only wanted a burger and a drink but it was cheaper for a full meal so I got the chips too', he confessed.

Dundonald's oldest joyrider arrested

Dundonald's oldest joyrider and his girlfriend had a lucky escape today when the stolen car they were driving flipped onto its side.

Cecil Astra, 83, was dipping the clutch on a stolen Honda when he suddenly lost control of the vehicle.

The geriatric hood managed to crawl through the passenger side window with his girlfriend, Shelly-Anne Nova, 81, still trapped inside.

Astra told the PSNI he was unable to see over the waist band of his trousers and clipped a kerb which caused the vehicle to topple.

Officers believe that Cecil may have been under the influence of several substances including Viagra and Fisherman's Friends.

Cecil broke into his first car (a Ford Anglia) in 1939 when he was just 6-years-old.

By the time he was 11 he'd been arrested fourteen times and was a father-of-two.

Astra and his girlfriend are members of a local gang who refer to themselves as the 'Dunlady Hoods'.

The gang are residents at Dunlady Nursing Home but have been escaping from the facility after 'lights out' to engage in illegal street racing.

Terrorized locals claim they've witnessed the old hoods rampage about the streets on mobility scooters at speeds of up to 10mph.

There are videos on Astra's YouTube account which show the gang in action and bragging about their antics.

In one clip, Cecil is stood beside a burnt out Rascal 388 deluxe mobility scooter shouting 'Lock it or lose it ya ball-begs - yeoooo'.

Devastated Dundonald woman's landmark birthday not marked by bed sheet hanging off high school bridge

A distraught Dundonald woman's family have refused to hang a bed sheet displaying a handwritten message over the high school footbridge to mark her 30th birthday , it has emerged.

30-year-old Kelly-ann MacDramagh fully expected to see a large white sheet exhibiting a scrawled birthday message in her honour whilst making her daily commute this morning.

However, to Kelly-ann's dismay, the only banner on display was one demanding the release of Tommy Robinson.

Having a bed sheet birthday message slung over the high school bridge is as much of a Dundonald rite of passage as being fingered in the Moat Park or suffering a first-degree burn on the Indianaland Free-Fall.

And Kelly-ann is heartbroken that neither friends or family 'bothered their holes' to do so.

"It doesn't even feel like my 30th nii", sobbed Kelly-ann.

"Cos let's face it, see unless there's a tattered bed sheet with 'Happy 30th Kelly-ann' written on it hangin' aff the high school bridge, was it even your birthday in Dundanal at all?", she quizzed.

But her family were adamant that unlike benefit fraud and criminality, this was one Dundonald tradition they wouldn't be adhering to.

"Sure how could I get up there with my vertigo, or her da with his back, or her we bro'rer with his anxiety?", questioned her mother Sylvia.

'What overcrowding?' ask Glider bosses

Glider-mania gripped Belfast yesterday with commuters eager to test out the new service after years of perpetual roadworks and traffic jams.

But Glider bosses moved swiftly to dismiss rumours that their new bendy buses are overcrowded.

Scores of disgruntled passengers said they were left stranded at stops along the Newtownards Road when jam-packed buses drove past them.

However, Translink bosses described the claims as: 'A lotta aul ballix'.

'There's plenty of fucking room', gasped Inspector Alexander Dennis while punching his way through a human crush.

'You don't hear any of them complaining', he said while pointing at four pensioners pressed up against the windscreen like 80s Garfield car window toys.

'Big deal. A few people might have to wait on the next bus. There'll be one in a couple of hours or so', he quipped, while giving a two-fingered to salute to a group of drenched school children at the bus stop.

It wasn't all negativity though as some passengers enjoyed their first Glider experience.

84-year-old Ethel Fossil who sleeps about 3 hours per day and has nothing better to do, said she hopped on the Glider 'for a wee nosy'.

'By 7am I'd been to the shops for the papers and had the whole house cleaned. I was just wondering how the fuck I was getting the rest of my day in when I remembered I was entitled to free travel'.

'So I decided to take a wee race down to Wyse Byse on the new purple bus to buy some shite I'll give away the next time somebody visits me', explained Ethel.

Meanwhile, Naomi Long has taken to social media to express her displeasure at the congestion the new bus lanes are causing.

Could be worse Naomi. At least you don't have to try to get to work in that traffic.

Face of Christ appears in Dundonald woman's Kit Kat Chunky

People all over the world see images of Jesus Christ in many things. Clouds, rocks, even toast.

But according to reports, a woman in Dundonald is the latest to find an image of Jesus revealed in her chocolate bar.

Mary Magee, 46, from Hanwood, always has a Kit Kat Chunky along with her 10am cuppa. She told us, 'I have a wee Kit Kat in the mornings, that's my cheat meal'.

'I dunked it in my tea, then took a big bite and I couldn't believe what I saw. 'Jesus Christ I thought'. I stuck a photo of it on Facebook and loads of people were sharing it'.

Mary rang her friend Sylvia and asked her to have a look. Sylvia, however, was sceptical, observing that the image looked to her to be more like comedian Russell Brand. But Mary was convinced.

'I believe that God himself had sent it to me to prove that he exists and I should not give up my faith. Ok, so I say the odd fuck and drink four nights a week but I don't care, I know the truth'.

Mary has set up a Facebook page, where people can make bookings to meet the chocolate Jesus for £10 a go.

'I don't see why Jesus wouldn't come back to Dundonald. I know there's that aul joke about not being able to find three wise men or a virgin in the place but I think he'd fit in rightly'.

'He's a joiner, loves a drink and has two da's', concluded Mary.

DLA 'debagging' To Continue

The Dundonald Liberation Army has claimed that it will continue its campaign of 'debagging' anyone found to be engaging in antisocial behaviour.

Several men entered a house on the Ballyregan Road at about 19:20 GMT on Tuesday evening. A 20-year-old man was taken from the property at water pistol point and dragged up a nearby alley where he was viciously debagged.

The victim was found by a dog walker several hours later with his tracksuit bottoms around his ankles.

Local gossipmonger Sally Tattler, who was walking her pet Alsatian at the time, said, 'I was just taking our Sasha out for a shite when I noticed a fella halfway up my entry. The poor lad was lying there in a pair of union jack boxers that said 100% British Beef on them. He was crying out for his mammy'.

It is the latest in a spate of attacks, all of which are said to have been carried out by the DLA. The terror group released a statement last week which read, 'The DLA will seek to punish those within the community who are engaging in antisocial behaviour. This may include: not going to the bar with your mates on a Friday after work or playing Candy Crush whilst someone is trying to talk to you'.

The 20-year-old was taken to the nearby Ulster Hospital where he is said to be 'pure scundered' but his condition is not thought to be life threatening.

Rosepark Service Station ATM Voted No1 Place to Take a Pish in Dundonald

A cash machine in the vicinity of Ardcarn has been voted the most popular place in Dundonald to take a drunken slash a recent survey has revealed.

Local tabloid, 'The Dundonald Voyeur', conducted a poll amongst 1,000 of Dundonald's most notorious piss artists and found that the Rosepark ATM was the place they enjoyed spraying urine about the most.

Renowned bar fly Duncan D. Orderly told us, 'It's a nice wee corner there so it is. The peelers can't see your genitals if they're driving past and if anyone's coming up behind ye ya can just say you're checkin your balance'.

Every week thousands of disgusted patrons using the cash point must inhale the toxic odours radiating from the gallons of pish that have been doused over it.

Local gossipmonger Sally Tattler complained, 'It's pure boggin so it is. I went the other day ler to lift a tenner and the whiff hit me up the bake like a Chris Brown left hook'.

She added, 'I dunno what's in the pints these days but the pish smells like a combination of Sugar Puffs and rat sick'.

On the other hand, longsuffering wives and girlfriends say they're delighted that their partners are urinating in the streets.

Wee Sadie explained, 'Our Albert's a dirty F'er when he's had a few drinks. He's pished in the wardrobe that many times I've nicknamed him 'Narnia'.

Dundonald Chemist Runs 'Netflix & Pill' Promotion

A pharmacy on the Upper Newtownards Road is offering a promotional discount on the 'morning after pill' for randy young couples, it has emerged.

The Dundonald-based pharmacy noticed an increase in the amount of young women queued outside the doors at opening time who were 'lukin la pill'.
Since 2011, 'Netflix & Chill' has been a euphemism for animalistic unprotected sex with anyone willing to participate.

As a result, the Medicare branch, situated in Dundonald Village, has collaborated with media streaming giants Netflix to offer customers a package deal whereby they receive a month's free subscription along with their emergency contraception.

Pharmacist Phil McDruggan said, 'I would open the shutters on a Saturday morning and there would be a snaking queue of women clutching a bottle of Evian and their mascara looking like Alice Cooper's'.

One of those customers, Sally McTarty, called to a local man's house to watch a Jason Statham movie.

She recalls, 'I went round to Big Andy's fer Netflix & Chill. About 20 minutes in he gimme lat luk'.

'Next fing a know am gettin wheelbarrowed while Transporter 2 plays in la background'.

'So am down here lis morning to get la pill. Eight kids is enough'.

Not everyone is a fan of Netflix & Chill though. Nigel Monk actually wanted to watch a film and was pestered for sex by his wife. He moaned, 'I'd been looking forward to watching The Ozark all day. But about 20 minutes in she was licking my neck like a springer spaniel'.

'I had to watch it on the i-Pad in the spare room', he admitted.

Cautious Jack Steekington was determined not to get his Netflix & Chill partner pregnant.

He told us, 'She's bin uppa spout more times than Itsy Bitsy spider. So a drove her down here first fing lis mornin to make sure sha tuk it'.

Dundonald Gay Community Secretly Fearing Marriage Law

Hundreds of homosexual Dundonald men are secretly praying that the Northern Ireland Executive doesn't legalise same-sex marriage.

For years' gays have been able to blame their lack of commitment on state sponsored homophobia. However, with a sway in public opinion making a referendum look like a formality, many homosexuals fear they may have finally ran out of excuses.

Thirty-two-year-old flight attendant Julian Thompson from Cherryhill remarked, 'This is a bloody nightmare. I've been with Sean for five years and if this law changes he'll want a ring on his finger'.

He continued, 'It's not that I don't love him but I haven't even told my granny I like cock. Plus, if we fall out, would he get to keep half my stuff? Fuck that'.

Forty-one-year-old hairdresser Simon McSorely complained, 'We've really done it this time. All those bloody demonstrations and Pride parades. It was only a matter of time before they gave us what we wanted. Who in their right mind wants to be tied to the same saggy arsehole for thirty or forty years? We bought a Pug together. Is that not enough commitment for some people?'

Smug unhappily married straight man Barry Graham from the Valley in

Ballybeen Estate added, 'Slap it into them. Running around there with their nice clothes and three holidays a year. Now they get to experience the living hell us heterosexual people must endure!'

'Being straight isn't a choice either by the way! So why should I feel obligated to get married just because I don't like the dick?'

Internal investigation after McDonald's Drive-Thru gets order right

A County Down branch of McDonalds has launched an in-house enquiry after it emerged that they actually got a customer's order right.

McDonald's bosses have promised to investigate the allegations made yesterday by a shocked but satisfied patron, who arrived home to find that all of the items he'd asked for were inside the bag.

Big Ronnie MacDonald, 35, made the startling discovery after using the branch's famous Drive-Thru facility which prides itself on its '100% guarantee of a ballsed up order'.

Sammy told us, 'If the wife's working late, she'd often tell me to bring a Micky Dee's home. Usually she can't wait to open the bag and tell the kids that daddy forgot to ask for plain burgers'.

'So last night when I pulled up to the Drive-Thru window, this effeminate male with wispy sideburns like Andre the Giant handed over my food - which I forgot to check as usual'.

'When I arrived home, much to our shock and amazement, the staff managed to include everything I asked for. Furthermore, it was relatively warm and edible'.

'As you can imagine, I was straight on the phone to the manager. How dare I arrive home to find I'd received all the items I'd paid for! The person I felt for the most was my wife. She couldn't even give me a bollocking'.

McDonalds chose to voluntarily and immediately close the premises until they feel they're ready to fuck up orders again.

A statement read: 'The branch will be closed until the matter is resolved.

In the meantime, you could re-create the conditions at home by lifting food off your spouse's plate and hiding it'.

Ulster Hospital Claims 'Crocs Most Effective Form of Contraception'

The Ulster Hospital have today confirmed that Crocs are now a more effective form of contraception than sterilisation or castration. The hideous foam clogs will be available on the NHS with effect from 2017.

A study found that 99.7% of men were unable to attain an erection whilst looking at a woman who was wearing the despicable plastic shoe. Conversely, 99.8% of women said they'd rather feed their legs into a wood chipper than let a Croc wearing male within a 5-mile radius of their genitalia.

The rubber shoe is said to be particularly popular with men who have no interest in sex and with obese women who sweat profusely during even the least taxing of tasks.

Dr Richard Head explained, 'Wearing Crocs has become a type of Social Darwinism. Obviously anyone who wears them is a bit slow and due to the lack of any sexual contact, these morons will eventually become extinct, purifying the human race'.

Sweaty mum-of-five with greasy hair big Tracy said, 'I luv ma wee Crocs so a do. I usually stick lem on wif a pair of leggings that luk like they've been vacuum formed round ma legs'.

CEO of Crocs Inc Brad Hogan said, 'After some research in 2004, it became apparent that some people were more concerned with well-ventilated feet than having sex. We saw a niche in the market and exploited it fully. We sent a shipment of Crocs to China and solved their over-populating issues within a decade'.

When quizzed about the vent holes in the shoes Mr Hogan explained, 'That's where your dignity pours out'.

Kosy Club Gets Hipster Revamp

Local anti-social club 'The Kosy' has been re-launched as a trendy

Hipster bar called 'The Spaniel's Ear'.

Regulars of the pub got a shock this morning when the doors opened to reveal the chic interior and trendsetting new bar staff.

72-year-old Alfie Tippler was the pub's first customer of the day. He explained, 'I was there for opening time as usual but this morning I was greeted by some bearded ballix in a flannel shirt with some sort of samurai hair cut'.

He continued, 'I went up to the bar which was built out of pompous books that twats would read in public and asked for a pint of Harp. The bar man told me they no longer sold pints of lager and offered me craft Buckfast instead. He then served it to me in a glass baking bowl'.

Mr Tippler was equally perplexed when he tried to order his usual bacon burger and chips for lunch.

He told us, 'All I wanted was a burger and chips to eat while sat on a normal seat. They served my chips on a floor board and I couldn't even sit at the bar because they'd replaced the bar stools with pogo sticks'.

The biggest shock of all came when Mr Tippler went to the toilet. He recalls, 'When I went in for a slash they'd ripped the urinal out and replaced it with buckets on the floor.

'That's all well and good when you're sober. But the place will be like the fuckin' Fountains of Bellagio about half nine on a Saturday night'.

He added, 'There was some black fella sat on a stool in the corner trying to spray me and shouting 'No Armani no punani'. Then he tried to stroke me a pound for a Chupa Chup, so I told him to do one'.

New bar man Franklin Swank, who always wears a hat indoors, remains defiant about his decision to elongate his lobes.

He said, 'Walking around with a drooping, flapping hole in each ear shows total commitment to the Hipster movement. There might be a fishy aroma oozing from the decomposing flesh and it will inevitably require plastic surgery but it was definitely worth it'.

Not enough children drinking shandy warn community

leaders

Local community workers believe that an entire generation of children are in danger of steering clear of nicotine and alcohol addiction, unless immediate action is taken.

Davy Yardbird is worried that unless companies reintroduce the sale of low alcohol shandy drinks and 'sweetie cigarettes', many of Northern Ireland's school children might never experience the joy that accompanies a life of alcohol dependency and respiratory illness.

Products such as Top Deck and Shandy Bass were marketed to children in the United Kingdom from the 1960s to the 1980s by ruthless companies hoping to desensitize children, leading them to become heavy drinkers in adult life.

It was not an uncommon sight in 1986 to see children under eight drinking such beverages in the playground before returning to class.

A misty eyed Davy Yardbrush recalled, 'I remember we'd get let outside for fifteen minutes at break-time to let the teachers get a feg and backstab the poor children'.

'All the kids in the playground would neck a tin a Top Deck while watchin two stray Labradors ride the life clean outta each other'.

'The caretaker would come out and brain one of the dogs with a brush to break them up. But I remember one day my wee mate ran up and kicked la dog right on the lipstick. He was a raker so he was. How he ended up in jail I'll never know'.

Wee Jean from 'Down-le-Road' always bought her child candy-cigarettes when she got her own tobacco products.

She remembered, 'I used to nip in for 40 regal kingsize and get ma chile 20 sweetie fegs while I was there. I thought I was doin him a good turn because it'd stap him from smoking mine when I went to bed the wee shite'.

She continued, 'Now I buy them for my grandson. He's just turned 3 and he's on the menthol Incredible Hulks'.

Dundonald Women Over 30 Still Calling It Woolco

Startling new statistics by the Institute of Silly Studies have revealed that 97.9% of women over the age of thirty are still referring to Ards Shopping Centre as Woolco.

Despite the fact that the commercial premises were rebranded as Ards Shopping Centre during the late 90s, many women are refusing to acknowledge the change.

Big Ethel from Ballybeen told us, 'Every Saturday since the 70s I've gotta a taxi down to Ards to do a bitta shappin. When I rings the depo and they ask me where I'm going I say Woolco. They know what I mean straight away'.

She added, 'When la taxi driver asks me 'Where to luv?' I tell him Woolco as well. The tattoos on his forearms would lead to believe he's done a few people in in his day but he still has the manners not to correct me'.

Wee May from Tullycarnet also still refers to it as Woolco. She explained, 'Why wuda say Ards Shappin Centre? That's three words and Woolco is one. It's just cammin sense'.

She continued, 'It's the same with la shaps in Dundanal. I still get a taxi to Wellworse every Saturday, I don't care what ya call it nigh, it'll always be Wellworse to me'.

Dundonald Man 'On the Fegs' to Quit Vaping

A local man has started smoking tobacco cigarettes in order to wean himself off nicotine vapour, it has emerged.

Big 'Dopey' Dave Stewart, 26, inadvertently became addicted to nicotine when he started vaping just over a year ago.

Dave, a non-smoker, began vaping because 'all his mates were doing it' and through time became heavily dependent upon the vapour emitting electronic device.

The twenty-six-year-old's parents became concerned about their son's over-use of the e-cig and told him he should cut down.

After a brief consultation with the medical experts on his Facebook friends list and a quick pre-wank nosey on Google, Dave decided the best way to quit vaping was to start smoking.

Dave told us, 'I've managed to cut back on my vaping by smoking ten Sterling Menthol a day'.

When told that Nicotine was a highly addictive substance on a level comparable to heroin and cocaine, Dave replied, 'Awk that's a lotta ballix so it is.

'Sure I've been on the heroin for months and look at me the day? I drove the nephew to school just fine'.

And when informed that smoking tobacco was more harmful than vaping Dave snapped, 'Sure everything's bad for ye according to yousens. Drinking, McDanalds – next you'll be sayin' sniffin' glue is bad for ye!'.

Dundonald man spontaneously combusts in Ice Bowl Free-Fall accident

A Dundonald man burst into flames today after he went down the Indianaland 'free-fall' wearing a short sleeved t-shirt and a pair of jeans.

Father of two, Robbie Burns, was visiting the indoor playground with his young family when he decided to recapture his youth and take a trip down the giant 30ft slide.

Against the better advice of his 'scundered' girlfriend and concerned members of staff, Mr Burns dangled his legs over the edge and attempted to whip up a round of applause from completely disinterested patrons.

The extrovert experienced a sudden bout of anxiety and was contemplating abandoning the idea completely when he was pushed in the back by his 6-year-old son.

The 32-year-old foolishly put his hands against the slide which generated a loud squeaking noise as his flesh rubbed fiercely against the uncompromising plastic backboard.

As he gathered momentum, Mr Burns began to smoke before bursting into flames completely.

By the time he'd reached the bottom all that remained was a pile of smouldering ash and small badge which read 'I conquered the free-fall'.

His long-suffering girlfriend said, 'He always was a dickhead. Everywhere we went he always had to be the centre of attention and make a spectacle of himself'.

She continued, 'Ok he's dead. But on the plus side I'm expecting a hefty cheque from the life insurance - and I've just saved myself a few bob on getting the fucker cremated!'

3 PALATIKS

NI to legalise recreational sex

Following Canada's decision to legalise recreational marijuana, Northern Ireland's politicians have announced their plans to legalise recreational sex, according to reports.

The move comes following criticism of Northern Ireland's political leader's perceived 'draconian' attitudes towards issues such as gay marriage and abortion.

A statement made on behalf of Northern Ireland's political parties read:

'As part of an ongoing initiative to make Northern Ireland one of the world's most progressive regions, it is our intention to legalise recreational intercourse between same sex couples'.

'No longer will the old rumpy-pumpy be reserved for procreation purposes only'.

'We would encourage those folk of matching sexual orientation to 'have it off' at least twice a month'.

Arlene Foster said the proposal was yet another example of the forward-thinking policies of the Democratic Unionist Party.

'I do enjoy a spot of how's your father', blushed Arlene.

'And this law will enable all my constituents to get their leg over on a more regular basis'.

However, the news caused uproar in Ballymena where doggy-style intercourse is still illegal.

The TUV's Jim Allister launched a scathing attack on the other parties for their 'debauchery'.

Allister, who claims 'the female orgasm is nothing but a myth', has called on those in his constituency to 'refrain from engaging in unnecessary sexual activity'.

Meanwhile, man-eating sex-pot Naomi Long has welcomed the news.

'Get her bucked', yelled Long while handing out free samples of KY Jelly outside her East Belfast offices.

Gladiator's Travelator to solve Irish border issue

A resolution to Brexit's thorniest issue has been found after the UK and EU agreed to put the infamous 'Travelator' on the Irish Border.

After a round of crucial talks between European leaders, it was decided that the gruelling obstacle from television's 'Gladiators' was a preferred alternative to a hard border.

Delegations from all those involved in talks emerged from the summit with their arms aloft after resolving the contentious issue.

'After hearing that a hard border could potentially kick-off World War 3, we decided that the Travelator was a far better option', explained Theresa May whilst attempting the Swish dance.

'Anyone hoping to enter the UK will have to conquer the moving walkway'.

'We believe this will be particularly effective in keeping out the fat, the disabled and elderly who would undoubtedly be a huge drain on the NHS', added May.

It was also confirmed that 86-year-old Scottish referee John Anderson from the Gladiators television series will be brought out of retirement to oversee any immigration attempts.

'Anyone hoping to legally enter the UK will not only have to scale the Travelator but must do so whilst being pursued by Gladiator villain Wolf', explained May.

'Oh yes, you'll be chased up a steep escalator by a growling man in Lycra with a balding soft-perm. That's how hard it'll be to enter the UK now', chuckled the Prime Minister.

'Awooooogaaaah', shouted John Fashanu.

Gay cake called as witness in court case

The homosexual dessert at the centre of the 'gay cake' row was called to testify in the High Court discrimination case this morning.

The cake, real name Simon Brown, was cross-examined by the lawyers representing both Ashers Bakery and Gay Rights activist Gareth Lee.

The poor pudding broke down in tears while recounting his version of events leading up to today's landmark legal trial.

'Jesus didn't want me for a bloody sunbeam' sobbed the cake in front of the jurors.

The cake revealed how its life had been turned upside down by the media circus generated by the case.

'Ach, the past four years have been a flipping nightmare'.

'Sure I couldn't even show my bake on Union Street without a pack of melters asking for selfies', the cake added.

The cake also revealed how all the attention from case put a tremendous strain on his relationship with a chocolate eclair called Dave.

'Dave didn't like all the attention I was getting. Every time we went on a night out he'd go full-Mariah cos he'd think someone was flirting with me'.

In the end it all became too much and they called time on their relationship after 4 years together.

'Oh mummy, I miss Dave like f**k', wept the cake.

'Swear on my hair, if it wasn't for that bloody court case we'd still be a couple'.

As the news broke this morning, hundreds of people rushed to social media to row in the comments sections of online news articles.

Supporters of both parties flooded our newsfeeds with crucifixes and rainbow flags as word of the verdict spread.

When asked if it was relieved the case was finished the cake said, 'Thank the Lord it's all over'.

Possible MLA sighting at Stormont a hoax

Rumours of a possible MLA sighting at Stormont have been exposed as an elaborate hoax, it has emerged.

Weed-smoking paranoid crackpot, Connor Spiracy (36), made the startling claim that he saw a Northern Irish MLA at work and had photographic evidence to back it up.

However, the man's lies were exposed after a careful examination of the evidence by experts at Dundonald Looniversity.

The flat-earther said he captured the footage on the grounds of Stormont and the images he uploaded to social media were shared thousands of times around the globe.

'I was skinning a jay, when suddenly, I heard a rustling in the bushes', recalled Connor.

'When much to my surprise, an MLA emerged from the thicket'.

'It was a well-rested looking creature, relaxed'.

'But when it spotted the Stormont Parliament Buildings in the distance it became agitated and disappeared back into undergrowth', he added.

Many esteemed Northern Irish scientists discount the existence of MLAs and consider it to be a combination of folklore, misidentification and hoax.

Another local researcher, Anthony P. O'logist, has spent the last twelve months of his career searching for MLAs.

'These magnificent beasts usually hibernate for the whole of December but for some reason they've remained dormant for over twelve months', said Anthony.

However, Belfast zoologist Big Steeky Irwin believes the latest supposed sighting is nothing more than another hoax.

'There is no such thing as an MLA', blasted Steeky.

'No data other than fabricated material has ever been presented'.

'MLAs sighted near Stormont. What next? A Civil Servant at his desk after 12 noon on a Friday? A UTV programme that's not about rambling in rural Ulster? Gerry Adams WAS in the 'ra?', questioned Steeky.

Britain First chase Dracula out of Ballymena

A video began circulating on social media yesterday which appeared to show heroic members of Britain First chasing a ghastly ghoul out of a small County Antrim town.

Brave leader Paul Golding and three associates confronted the blood-sucking fiend in the street about its residential status or whether the creature was in receipt of any benefits.

But before they could extract an answer from the shapeshifting demon, it morphed into a large bat then rose into the skies above with the Britain First posse in hot pursuit.

'I'm gonna drive this steak into his heart', yelled Golding into the camera while holding a blood-dripping Filet Mignon aloft.

Golding said that he and his organisation were invited to the town by local residents who have been terrorised by the evil Nosferatu.

'Fangs but no fangs, 'County' chops, time to f**k off back home', he added.

One local woman welcomed the fact that Britain First had visited the town after bearing witness to some antisocial behaviour from the migrant community.

'I was walking my dog the other day when this big Romanian woman wearing a Kappa tracksuit and a headscarf just dropped her bags and took a big shite in the park. That there carryon's stinking, so it is'.

Another local, Sam Stoker, claims he wasn't aware of the vampire's presence in the town but wouldn't object as long as it behaved itself.

'He can drink my blood but if he touches my pint I'll knock his ballix in', said Sam.

Dressing gown/House coat debate 'bigger threat to Good Friday Agreement than Brexit'.

A row over whether we should say 'Housecoat' or 'Dressing Gown' has been described as Northern Ireland's biggest political crisis yet.

It comes amid speculation the DUP and Sinn Féin are close to agreeing a deal to restore devolved government here.

Talks between the parties descended into farce when a slanging match broke out over the proper name for the loose fitting robe, worn by those who spend unusually long periods at home doing fuck all.

The garment is normally worn before getting dressed in the mornings and after getting undressed in the evenings.

However, if you go to Connswater Shopping Centre around 12 noon on a Tuesday, you'll see lots of women wearing them while buying their groceries.

Unionist MLAs wanted the piece of clothing to be called a 'Dressing Gown'.

Meanwhile, Sinn Fein were adamant the garment should be referred to as a 'Housecoat'.

'I don't wear one myself. My house is roasting with the wood pellets burning day and night', explained DUP leader Arlene Foster.

'But as far as I'm aware the correct term for the robe is 'Dressing Gown'. You wouldn't call slippers bloody 'House Shoes', now would you?', said Foster.

'Listen til all the snobs calling it a 'Dressing Gown'. It's bloody shackin', snapped Sinn Fein leader Michelle O'Neill.

'Next they'll be callin' shite roll 'toilet paper', fegs 'cigarettes' or gravy rings 'doughnuts'. The only doughnuts up this neck of the woods are done in a stolen Vauxhall Astra outside Divis Flats', she added.

Prime Minister Theresa May and Taoiseach Leo Varadkar weighed into the debate in the hope of reaching an amicable solution.

'In the interests of respect and equality, similar to Derry/Londonderry, they should call it a 'Housecoat-Dressing Gown', reasoned May.

Scientology 'fleg' spotted in Belfast

A 'fleg' supporting the Church of Scientology has been spotted up a lamppost in Belfast.

It is understood that either Themuns or Usuns are showing solidarity with the controversial organisation which has been passing leaflets around the city in recent days.

It is the latest in a series of strange 'flegs' unfurled by locals who love nothing more than hijacking foreign disputes or aligning themselves with contradictory causes.

Tom Cruise

Hollywood A-list weirdo Tom Cruise appeared in a YouTube video this afternoon to express his appreciation on behalf of the Church of

Scientology.

'I stand shoulder to waist band with our Northern Irish brothers today', beamed the 4ft actor.

'They are showing their solidarity with us Scientologists against the evil dictator Xenu, who 75 million years ago brought people to this earth and then killed them with hydrogen bombs'.

There's been a scramble by both sides of the community here to affiliate themselves with the Scientologists.

Dessie Dent from the New Lodge area was keen to ally with the Scientologist's.

'They're a bit like the Catholic Church, wealthy and secretive but without the child abuse'.

'They might be a pack of weirdos but when it comes to the border poll we're gonna need all the help we can get'.

But Big 'Turk' Young who lives on the Newtownards Road was convinced that Scientologists were loyal to the crown.

'Sure was your man Tom Cruise working with MI6? Could'a swore I watched something on Netflix about that?'.

'Not another fucking religion'

But not everybody was enthused by the sight of a Church of Scientology standard flapping in the wind.

'That there's just what we need so it is', sighed Atheist Davy Middleton. 'Another fucking church'.

'I hate everything to do with organized religion - except their holidays and days off work'.

Bitter ballixes arguing about Israel & Palestine... again

Prods and Catholics in Northern Ireland took a break from their own daily ethno-nationalist squabbles to weigh into a row over a sectarian conflict between Jews and Arabs today.

It's the latest in a series of slanging matches between people who have the ability to turn every event, either domestic or foreign, into an Orange & Green debate.

Big 'Turk' Young (43), from the loyalist Albertbridge Road wrote a Facebook post in which he encouraged the Israeli troops to 'get stuck inta lem'.

'The Israeli ones are like our ones here, aren't they not?', quizzed Turk who initially thought the Gaza Strip was a Rangers kit from 1996.

'To be honest with ye, it's all a bit over my head but anything to wind the Taigs up, eh?', he chuckled while hoisting an Israeli flag up a lamp post.

Meanwhile, wee Dessi Dent (47) from Ardoyne was just as vociferous in his support for the Palestinians.

'I've a lot in common with them'uns, so I do. My land is illegally occupied by a foreign invader, the Huns. Palestinians grew up in the West Bank - I grew up in Hydebank and helped rob the Northern Bank', explained Dessi.

When asked for his thoughts on Hamas, Dessi replied, 'Dunno mate, never tried it. Is that not somethin' froots dip their Doritos in?'.

Meanwhile the owner of The Rock Bar's 'head is melted' over which flag to unfurl before NI kickoff against Israel.

Pope Francis spotted on Knock Road

Pope Francis has been spotted driving along the Knock Road and waving at gobsmacked onlookers, it has emerged.

The sight of the Popemobile cruising through East Belfast brought traffic to a standstill with many people unable to believe their eyes.

A mix-up in the Pontiff's itinerary is being blamed for the unannounced visit to Belfast after he failed to appear at the Roman Catholic pilgrimage site in the village of Knock, County Mayo.

The motorcade made its way along the Newtownards Road until it stopped outside the Con Club.

Staff were left in a state of 'total shack' when the supreme pontiff asked if they were still serving lunch.

One eyewitness claims that his holiness and his entourage held hands and said a prayer as soon as the waitress arrived back with their chicken goujons and chips.

At first they believed it was an elaborate hoax but it quickly became apparent it was indeed the 266th Bishop of Rome

'I thought it was some fellas on a Stag party taking the piss', recalls barfly Basher Stewart.

'But they were talkin' in I-talian and were old as aul fuck. So I Googled a picture of the Pope and sure enough, it was him'.

'I text a few of the lads to tell them the Pope was in the Con Club eating chicken goujons but they told me to sober up and fuck off'.

#WeDeserveBetter say people who vote for same old shite every time

As Northern Ireland rapidly approaches 589 days without a functioning assembly, the people are saying they deserve better.

This is despite the fact nearly all of them vote for the same arseholes during every election.

It's just six days left until the milestone which will see us overtake Belgium's 2010-2011 record time without a functioning government.

And now the very idiots who elected these politicians are feeling hard done by.

Even though the majority of these people would have you believe they vote for moderate parties, they're exposed as big lying bastards as soon as they ballots are counted.

'I don't want a United Ireland', confessed one female closet DUP voter.

'Scandals – Schmandals. Sure, in some sort of utopian democracy I could base my decision on things like health, economic and education policies but that's impossible'.

'You honestly think Emily Wilding Davison threw herself under a horse so I could stick an 'X' beside Sammy Wilson's name? But needs must. Those bastards will not get their way'.

A closet Sinn Fein voter told us: 'I want a United Ireland'.

'Any Prod ever asks me on a work night out who I vote for and I just about keep a straight face while saying SDLP'.

'The reunification of the 32 counties is so close, we can almost smell it. When it comes to the border poll, we'll have the LGBT community on our side, the Poles and Romanians too – in fact just about every minority group the DUP have insulted and we pretend we care about'.

'You honestly think I care if two lads from Ballybeen Estate can ride each other in Holy Matrimony? Na, but a vote's a vote!'

The Dundonald Liberation Army have set up their own protests which will be called #WeDeserveEverythingWeGet or #SlapItUpYe

Olly Murs releasing album for Republican prisoners after Féile gig

Olly Murs will donate the proceeds of a new album to the families of Republican prisoners, it has emerged.

The English singer-songwriter claims he was inspired to do so after performing in Falls Park as part of the Féile an Phobail 30th anniversary celebrations.

The 34-year-old enjoyed his stay in West Belfast so much that he stayed on for Sunday night's Wolfe Tones gig.

At one point he was spotted in the crowd draped in an Irish Tricolour and chanting 'Ooh ah uppa 'Ra'.

Now the former X-Factor contestant has promised to ease the burden on the families of Republican prisoners that be believes have been 'unlawfully interned'.

Murs hopes the album will raise awareness about, 'The continued use of unjust powers by the British government to revoke a person's licence without producing any evidence of wrongdoing which is an affront to human rights and natural justice'.

The Essex-born crooner says the new album will be a reworking of some of his biggest hits but with a 'socialist republican vibe'.

Tracks on the new album will include:

The Troubles- maker,

Heart Skips a Punishment Beating,

Republican Army of Two,

Marching Seasons,

Stevie Nolan Knows,

And

Up (the Ra)

The move comes after American rapper and producer will.i.am has announced plans to collaborate with the Gertrude Star Flute Band on a new album under the pseudonym Prince will.i.am of Orange.

Review: 'Trouts will be sauté', a cookbook by Gerry Adams

We've been treated to a sneak preview of the new cookbook which is really causing a stir, 'Trouts will be sauté', by former Sinn Fein president Gerry Adams.

The veteran republican's head has filled a few stockings over the years and now he's releasing his first cookbook just in thyme (pun intended) for Christmas.

The Louth TD revealed his plans at Féile an Phobail in West Belfast on Monday night where dozens of people were intimidated into pre-ordering the book.

'Gerry faced a few grillings in Castlereagh but little did we know he was a deft hand in the kitchen'.

'He's a very accomplished crook, eh, I mean cook', said a Sinn Fein spokesman.

They say never judge a book by its cover but when it's Gerry Adams holding a ceramic mortar and pedestal, it's hard not to.

But the West Belfast man's explosive range of culinary concepts will take some beating.

There's a handy 'Green in 15' section for those eating 'on the run'.

He's also provided a handy guide to eating a sirloin without the use of a steak knife.

However, it's his traditional recipes with a socialist republican twist that make this an essential guide for nationalist nutrition.

Dishes like 'Bangers & Sash', 'Fuck a l'orange', 'We haven't Scone away y'know' and 'Gerry Mandarin Orange Jelly', will have you begging for mercy.

'Trouts will be sauté', priced £19.16, will be available on Amazon next week.

However, when pressed for a comment about the imminent release Mr Adams said: 'I was never in the kitchen. I totally refute that allegation'.

Michelle O'Neill taking a break from taking a break after leg break

Sinn Fein Northern Ireland leader Michelle O'Neill is taking a break from taking a break after breaking her leg, her party has confirmed.

'Michelle O'Neill is going off on the sick 'til her leg's better', said a party spokesman in a brief statement.

O'Neill, who's already enjoyed over 500 days off on full pay, immediately informed Stormont she'd be off for another six months.

'Looking forward to sittin' on my hole, binging on Jezza Kyle and Judge Rinder', beamed O'Neill while scratching her broken leg with a knitting needle.

The circumstances surrounding the nature of the leg break remain a closely guarded secret at Sinn Fein HQ. Although we can definitely rule out it being an accident at work.

Fresh rumours circulating this morning suggest it was the result of a punishment beating at the behest of Gerry Adams after O'Neill failed her GCSE Irish Oral exam, again.

A row broke out yesterday between MLAs who were asked to sign her cast but couldn't agree if their get well messages should be written in Gaelic, Ulster Scots or English.

The former Stormont Health Minister has also called upon her party to stop pursuing the reunification of Ireland whilst she gets her leg mended for free on the NHS.

UN threatens to send NI politicians to Zimbabwe unless order is restored

The United Nations have threatened to send Northern Ireland's politicians to Zimbabwe unless the people there accept the result of Monday's election, it has emerged.

Widespread violence erupted when parliamentary results gave victory to the ruling Zanu-PF party even though the MDC opposition alliance insists its candidate, Nelson Chamisa, beat the incumbent President Emmerson Mnangagwa.

It's the first election since the removal of Robert Mugabe, who is rumoured to have died in 1997 but ruled until 2017 with the aid of some 'Weekend at Bernie's' style antics.

After troops opened fire on protesters there have been international calls for restraint.

And now the United Nations has threatened to replace Zimbabwe's political leaders with their Northern Irish counterparts unless everybody there gets their shit together.

"Imposing economic sanctions on the region could lead to a humanitarian disaster. So we've decided to charter a plane filled with Stormont MLAs instead", explained UN Secretary General António Guterres.

"The Zimbabwean electorate only thing think witnessed political corruption. Wait until they get a load of these bone idle self-serving freeloaders".

"Some of these bastards make Robert Mugabe look like Nelson Mandela", he added.

As the news reached Harare, rioters hugged in the streets and sobbed at the prospect of Jim Allister & co making decisions that shaped their children's future.

"Fuck that, bring back Mugabe", were the cries from the throng of protesters.

Parades Commission Ban Belfast Gay Pride

The 28th annual Belfast Gay Pride march has been thrown into disarray after it was barred from parading along the City Centre, it has emerged.

The ruling was made after three men in drag breached a Parades Commission determination by singing Liza Minnelli songs while passing a church in the City Centre last year.

Several nights of cat-fighting took place after that march was stopped, with scores of police officers getting their hair 'trailed' and 'scrabbed to bits'.

The LGBT activists have maintained a continuous presence and have set up a 'camp protest' outside the City Hall.

One activist, Gerald Fitzpatrick, told us:

'The parades commission has shown why it is a failed approach yet again'.

'So what if some of the boys belted out 'All That Jazz' after a few gins? It's a free country flip sake'.

Crisis talks have been held between the Parade's Commission and LGBT representatives with the situation about to go 'totally Britney 2007', according to sources.

In an unusual move, the commission offered Pride goers the ultimatum of playing no Liza Minnelli or Erasure music between Donegall Street and Union Street or having no parade at all.

One concerned resident Rab Rouser, who doesn't live near the church but wades into these debates to whip up tension, told us:

'I was on my way to get my granny a bottle of milk when suddenly I was surrounded by a troupe of flamboyantly dressed men singing Gloria Gaynor songs'.

He added, 'A person should be able to go about their ordinary business, which may include a lot of unnecessary trips to the shop for milk, without the fear of being serenaded by a pack of beautiful men'.

Amidst the chaos, Pride organisers have appealed for 'glam'.

Disused Stormont set to become a sunbed shop

Stormont is set to re-open as a tanning salon, according to reports this morning.

The disused parliament buildings, vacant since 10th January 2017, have finally found a new occupier and will officially open for business next week.

The new solarium called 'Black and Tans', promises to provide its customers 'with that perfect red-raw shade for the summer rioting season'.

Proprietor Helen McMelter, announced the news earlier with a Facebook post which read: 'My new beds are arriving l'mara. It all seems real nai'.

It's all the result of an online poll in which Northern Irish taxpayers were asked to suggest new uses for the building following the collapse of the NI assembly.

32.5% suggested setting fire to the building and shovelling their hard earned money into the flames, whilst 0.5% advocated the idea of allowing Stormont to lie dormant indefinitely, all of whom were MLAs.

However, 67% of voters thought another sunbed shop was just what the Newtownards Road needed.

Acquiring 'a tawn' is a hobby enjoyed by thousands of men and women in Belfast and the majority believe 'another wee sunbed shap' is just what the city needs.

Despite this, hundreds of people free from the shackles of employment protested outside the parliament buildings yesterday.

But local woman Melanie O'Maugh, whose back has more moles than an MI5 infiltrated IRA unit and likes to expose herself to UV radiation on a daily basis, told us:

'Stormont's been fulla hot air and tubes for decades. I don't see what the big fuss is about'.

DeLorean Accidentally Takes Northern Ireland Back to the 80s

Dunmurry's last remaining time machine has accidentally transported Northern Ireland back to the 1980s, it has emerged.

The incident occured when a group of youths hijacked a DeLorean DMC-12 which was driving through South West Belfast in the early hours of this morning.

The vehicle was on its way to a local Comic-Con when it was approached by a hooded-teen who ordered its drivers out of the car.

Eye-witnesses claim the carjackers reached a speed of 88mph which activated the vehicle's flux-capacitor after they generated a power of 1.21 'here's-me-wats?'.

As a result, the entire province was sucked into a black hole altering the space-time continuum which transported Northern Ireland back to the 1980s.

The RUC arrested the carjackers after observers saw a vehicle arrive in an implosion of plasma and a flash of light.

Martin 'Marty' McFly (17) and Emmett 'Doc' Brown (51), were arrested at the scene and taken away for further questioning.

They were transported to Castlereagh Holding Centre for a 'good talking to', with charges including 'An effort to rekindle The Troubles', 'Indoctrination of Children with Failed Ideologies' and 'A reintroduction of Bloody Pubic Hair'.

Both men deny the charges and claim they were only on the way to the shop to fetch their respective grandmothers a carton of milk.

Speaking from his cell in the Maze, Marty McFly told us, 'A person should be able to go about their day-to-day routine, which might include unnecessary time-travel for milk, without the fear of being brutalised by the Royal Ulster Constabulary - whoever the fuck they are'.

In better news, we still have to look forward to the 82 & 86 World Cups.

Lost North Korean Nuclear Sub turns up at Portavogie Harbour

A nuclear submarine containing North Korean leader Kim Jong-un washed up in a small fishing port on the Ards Peninsula, according to reports.

The Gangnam Style singer, 33, was testing out the new vessel when he and his crew got lost somewhere around Australia and somehow ended up in Portavogie.

Portavogie is a tiny village and port which lies within the Borough of Ards. The 2011 Census revealed it had a population of 2,122, all of which are cousins.

The crew were greeted by curious locals after rumours began circulating around the village that a mysterious 'iron whale' was spotted at the harbour.

'T'was the darndest thing I ever saw', said local Billy Ray McAuley. 'I told my brother-uncle Bubba there was an iron fish in the harbour and he almost pooped in his dungarees'.

Kim and his crew were taken on a tour of the village by residents, taking in sights including the old movie set where 'Deliverance' was shot in 1972.

The Korean supreme leader sampled local delicacies including salted herring, scampi and incest. He was then treated to a rendition of 'Dueling Banjos' by a lad with a large head and almond shaped eyes.

Before setting sail the Koreans were given a map and some supplies by locals. Kim Jong-un reportedly enjoyed his time there so much, he had the town's motto 'she's only your ma from the front' tattooed on his leg.

When news of the episode spread to the White House, president Donald Trump said that Portavogie would be met with 'fire and fury they haven't seen since the 11th night last year'.

Trump turns attention to solving Ballybeen-Tullycarnet conflict

Following the success of the summit talks between Donald Trump and North Korean leader Kim Jong-un, the US President has vowed to bring an end to the long running Ballybeen-Tullycarnet conflict.

Trump is hoping to succeed where the UN has failed and finally bring peace and stability between BT16 and BT5

'That's the ultimate deal,' he told the Wall Street Journal in an interview outside a South Korean massage parlour.

And many commentators believe Trump could be the man to strike that deal as he fits the type of profile the locals can relate to.

'He has a blonde bouffant hair-do, a bright orange tan and is a bit of a tyrant. Why, he's practically an East Belfast man', explained one White House source.

The ongoing struggle between Ballybeen and Tullycarnet began in the mid-20th century with both claiming to be the hardest estate on the outskirts of Belfast.

However, a series of 'fair-digs' between men, women, children and dogs from opposing sides proved to be inconclusive.

Ballybeen was seen as the more progressive housing estate when in 1983 they granted women the right to travel on the inside of the No8 bus and also earn equal pay with donkeys.

Tullycarnet has been more conservative and only last year granted men the permission to cry at funerals.

There have been claims of bias levelled at Castlereagh Council when they chose to build amenities such as the Ice Bowl, Pirates Adventure Golf and The Omniplex Cinema right on Tullycarent's doorstep.

'They have an all-weather pitch and we've Brookies field covered in white dog shite', moaned one Ballybeen resident.

'It's time for the beleaguered people of Ballybeen to wake up to the scale of this discrimination'.

Air Force One is scheduled to arrive at George Best airport around 4pm when the President will be whisked away to spend the night in a traffic jam in Dundonald Village before meeting representatives from both communities in the morning.

Asked if there was anything in particular about the visit he was looking forward to, Trump replied, 'Going down the free-fall in Indianaland, folks'.

There are no plans to visit Newtownards as it's one of the places Trump described as a shit-hole nation.

Fury as drunken DLA men receive on the rum letters

Letters given by the British Government to members of the Dundonald Liberation Army telling them they were not wanted for crimes committed whilst under the influence of Captain Morgan's rum were 'questionably unlawful' Lisburn City Council has declared today.

The County Down freedom fighters have been terrorising the local community with their drunken antics for several years but have always managed to avoid prosecution.

People were unsure why until the DLA's 'tap mawn', Davy 'The Venezuelan' Taylor was landed in court for urinating against an ATM outside a local Spar.

'Big Davy was lifted for exposing his penis in public', revealed our source.

'Embarrassingly, the judge dismissed the case for lack of evidence', said the source whilst wagging his baby finger.

But now it seems the real reason for The Venezuelan's release from custody has nothing to do his tiny manhood but instead a government pardon.

Davy's 'right-hawnd-mawn', John 'Horse' McCracken, managed to avoid paying any child maintenance because he was also in possession of an 'on the rum' letter.

McCracken, often referred to by his comrades as 'Father Abraham' on account of the amount of sons he's fathered, was pursued for child support by one woman who claims the DLA man is father to three of her nine children.

'The CSA had him by the balls but he said the only reason he rode me was cos he was on the Morgans', explained Kelly Joelene Campbell who answered the door in a Betty Boop nighty.

'So he whips out his 'on the rum letter' and now he doesn't have to pay a penny for his kids. Typical mawn. But never mind the CSA, karma will get him. I can hold my head high', she yelled.

Facebook police to replace PSNI

A newly formed online policing service is set to replace the PSNI, according to reports emerging this morning.

And the move has been welcomed by people who believe the PSNI has failed in just about every way imaginable.

The self-appointed online policing service will comprise of thousands of Facebook users and the essential criteria for new recruits will include: a smartphone; a decent WiFi connection and an unwavering determination to offer their opinion.

Minister for Justice and Equality, Charles Flanagan explained: 'When I checked my emails this morning I was invited to sign Big Sharon's petition to abolish the Policing Service of Northern Ireland'.

'It was Monday morning, I hadn't had my coffee yet and I thought, 'fuck it', so I disbanded the PSNI'.

'Much like the PSNI, it doesn't matter if you're Chucky Norris or Johnny Rambo, 50% of new officers will say 'Aitch' and the other 50% will say 'Haitch'.

The BAPS or Bakebook Arseholes Peeler Service will become effective immediately and could save the taxpayer around £500m a year.

New BAPS recruit Bobby Plod (47) explained what his new role would entail:

'You'll see me patrolling the comments section of all the local news stories 24/7. If I see anything I don't agree with, I'll reply to that person's post and haul them in for further questioning'.

'I haven't received any formal training per se, but I watched enough seasons of The Shield and CSI down the years'.

When asked if we could expect to see him walking the beat, kicking down drug-dealers doors or amputating the sofa from his arse at any point, Bobby said, 'Fuck that mate. The weather's shite and it's expected to piss down all week. I'll be keeping everyone safe from the comfort of my ma's spare room'.

No protests scheduled today – warns PSNI

Commuters have been warned to expect no unusual delays as Belfast prepares itself for a day without a protest.

'Unfortunately, it would appear that no one was offended by anything yesterday, so it's highly unlikely there'll be a protest today', Chief Constable George Hamilton told assembled journalists.

'We would appeal to anyone who felt even the slightest bit aggrieved by anything at all, to hastily arrange a public demonstration', he added.

Local MPs voiced their collective disapproval regarding the situation.

A joint statement, issued on behalf of all Northern Ireland's main political parties, read, 'We are unified in our belief that the people of this country are today not doing their best to ensure that people get home later than usual from work'.

'We would encourage anyone, especially those not bound by the shackles of employment, to find some reason to be offended and take to the streets. Now'.

'Flegs, Gay Cakes, Anti-Trump - surely there has to be one person out there offended today? Please? Anyone at all?'

Some of Northern Ireland's top celebrities such as Pete Snodden have vowed to immigrate to the Isle of Man unless a suitable protest can be found today.

Pete proclaimed, 'Like my good mates Bryan (Cranston) & Bob (Robert De Niro) who are in the extraordinary long-long process of moving to Canada after the election of Donald Trump, I too feel I would no longer be able to live in the country of my birth, if we as a nation are unable to find a reason to protest today'.

Zoe Salmon echoed Pete's sentiments by claiming, 'I don't think people are doing enough to be offended. Go online. People love being offended there. Go onto Facebook for fifteen minutes, you're bound to find something'.

Worldwide condemnation as Trump fails to recognize Lisburn as a shithole

REUTERS: Northern Ireland will issue a diplomatic protest to the United States over US President Donald Trump's refusal to acknowledge Lisburn as one of the planet's leading 'shitholes'.

During an Oval Office meeting on immigration last Thursday, Trump expressed frustration that Africans would rather die in a mass-shooting in the United States than somewhere else.

It is understood the President then proceeded to rhyme off a list of 'shithole nations' that were 'not worth invading' because they had 'no oil or money or stuff'.

However, Trump caused uproar across the globe when he omitted Lisburn from the aforementioned list.

Now Northern Irish politicians are demanding the US president apologises, after expressing their 'shack' at the omission.

We caught up with Green Party MLA Steven Agnew who was pawning his 72 inch 4K TV at a local Cash Converters.

He said, 'There is no other word one can use but racist. You cannot dismiss Lisburn as one of the world's biggest shitholes'.

Lisburn residents were equally dismayed by Trump's lack of recognition of their shiteness.

One local, Big Sandra Brown remarked, 'Lisburn's a bigger shithole than Haiti, Botswana or Senegal. How dare auld Tango-Tits forget about us'.

'Here, speaking of shitholes, look at his mouth when he talks. Looks like a puckered up bleached anus', she observed.

ISIS claims responsibility for new Daniel O'Donnell album

Isis has claimed responsibility for Daniel O'Donnell's 2017 album, 'Back Home Again', it has emerged.

Hot on the heels of taking responsibility for yesterday's mass shooting in Las Vegas, the terror group claimed they produced the album in an Iraqi studio towards the end of 2016.

The angry ninjas published a statement via the group's Amaq propaganda agency which read, 'Wee Daniel is a soldier of the Islamic State'.

Isis also claimed that the Donegal crooner 'converted to Islam several months ago' and had adopted the jihadi name 'Abu al-Ball-baghi'.

O'Donnell's career now spans over thirty years, during which time he has inflicted unspeakable suffering upon all those in the world with functioning ears.

However, his latest collection of softly sung sentimental shite, 'Back Home Again', is undoubtedly some of his most sinister work.

The news has come as a massive shock to O'Donnell's fans and fears are growing that hordes of pensioners may follow suit by turning to terror.

'There's a real worry that throngs of blue-rinsing grannies will declare jihad here in Ireland', claimed Paddy O'Doors of the Donegal Anti-Terroror Unit.

'We've already had one attempted attack today when an old lady mounted the pavement in a mobility scooter and drove toward pedestrians at speeds of up to 5mph', he added.

Donald Trump ready for Millisle attack

A confused Donald Trump claims the United States are prepared to wipe a small County Down village off the map.

In a tweet issued while taking a laboured shite, Mr Trump said: 'With the increasing threat of a Millisle attack, military solutions are now fully in place #WW3'.

The news sent shockwaves through the village which is known for its chip shops and caravan site sex-orgies.

A rambling Trump also contacted German chancellor Angela Merkel about imposing strict trade sanctions upon Millisle

During that call Trump threatened to cut off all trade with anybody who purchased goods in the bucket-and-spade resort.

'Anyone who buys a bag of dulse or a single stick of rock from those sons of bitches will be blacklisted', threatened Trump.

In light of Trump's threats, many people have decided to steer clear of the village.

'Usually, when there's fuck all to do on a Sunday, we take a wee race up to the Shankill-on-Sea', said Bangor man Adam Bombe.

'We go and get some chips or a stick-a-rack and eat them in the car while it pisses down with rain. But if your man Danald Trumpf is gonna start clauding nuclear weapons then I'll nat be back'.

'Hopefully nat though, there's enough f**kin rockets in Millisle', he added.

American-left tear down Philadelphia statue of man responsible for beating several black men

A group of protesters in Philadelphia have pulled down a statue of a man who was responsible for the brutal beating of several African-Americans, it has emerged.

The statue was dedicated to the Italian-American Rocky Balboa and stands outside the entrance to the Philadelphia Museum of Art, in Philadelphia, Pennsylvania.

The group gathered outside the museum around midday and a woman, free from the shackles of employment, tied a rope around Balboa's muscular neck.

The baying mob then pulled the rope, toppling the statue to the ground. Protesters can be seen kicking the inanimate effigy and celebrating its fall in videos taken by nosey bastards at the scene.

A Facebook event called for attendees to 'stand in solidarity with Charlottesville' and 'tear down this monument to white supremacy'.

'Balboa was a violent man who had links to Fascist groups in Italy', said one protestor.

'I remember my father showing me old VHS movies of this man brutalising several innocent black men. This monument is a constant reminder of the pain and suffering he inflicted upon the African-American community in Philadelphia', added another.

We tracked down one of Balboa's victims, Clubber Lang, to his mobile home on the outskirts of Pennsylvania. When asked if he had any thoughts on the tearing down of the statue, Land replied:

'Quit yo Jibber-jabber! Argh! If I ever catch you acting like a crazy fool on my porch again, you're gonna meet my friend pain!'.

Cliff Richards threatens to re-release 'We don't talk anymore' unless Stormont crisis resolved

Panic spread across the province this morning after it emerged that Cliff Richard is planning to re-release his No1 hit, 'We Don't Talk Anymore' – unless the main parties here can resolves their differences.

The toothy-warbler made the announcement via his Twitter account and sent thousands of beleaguered people into a frenzy.

'Haven't the people here suffered enough already?', questioned FannyWrecker69 under the Tweet.

'We've had The Troubles, Punishment Beatings, Lesser Spotted Ulster – now this? How much more can one country take?' he added

Shortly after the news broke, there was renewed optimism amongst the Northern Irish electorate, as all of the political parties appeared united in their hatred of Sir Cliff.

'I'd rather listen to a Willie McCrea album than that English b**tard', Tweeted Sinn Fein President Gerry Adams.

'It is time to re-engage in constructive dialogue before that buck-toothed Christian f**ker is on stage in the Waterfront is his gold waistcoat singing the Millenium Prayer', added the West Belfast man.

DUP leader Arlene Foster urged all the main parties to resolve their differences before the country is subjected to another rendition of Sir Cliff's 1979 synthpop smash.

'Come on da f**k lads, we've been on full-pay since November. Plus, that £1.5b from Theresa is still lying under Nigel Dodd's bed. We're minted. It's time to get back around the table and argue about the froots', Foster posted on her Bebo page.

A protest against the release of the song is planned for outside Belfast City Hall at 7pm this evening. Bono and Bob Geldof are waiting in the wings with their own song should Cliff pull out.

North Korean rocket hits Ballybeen

A housing estate on the outskirts of East Belfast was rocked to the core this morning when it was hit by a stray North Korean missile.

The long-range missile exploded on a patch of grass facing Davaar Avenue causing damage to the surrounding properties, although miraculously, no one was injured.

An announcement on North Korea state television said a Hwasong-14 missile was tested on Tuesday, overseen by leader Kim Jong-un who had just defeated a brick wall in a game of tennis in straight sets.

Unfortunately, a highly-intoxicated Kim Jong-un entered the wrong coordinates and the intercontinental ballistic missile (ICBM) landed in Ballybeen.

'Ballistic missile? Wait til my ma sees her washing. Then you'll see f**kin' ballistic mate. There's mud all over her whites', raged local woman Tracey-Ann.

'There are enough rockets around here love, we don't need any Korean ones', added Ginny, 71, who came out 'for a wee nosy' after the missile exploded.

Shortly after the explosion, a statement was released by the estate's own ballistics squad.

'The Ballybeen Rocket Team is on standby. We'll be sending a few incontinent rockets in your man Kim Jong-un's direction as soon as one of the lads gets back with an atlas'.

'I hear the capital of North Korea is Pyongyang. That's the same noise this frying pan will make when I whack Kim Jong-un around the bake with it', they added.

Bath-bomb explosion at East Belfast home

A leading Dundonald Liberation Army member is said to be in a stable condition in hospital after surviving a bath-bomb blast at his East Belfast home.

Reputed 'tap mawn' of the DLA, Davy 'The Venezuelan' Taylor, was soaking in the tub with a flannel over his face when a ball-shaped hard-packed mixture of fragrances and essential oils was tossed into his bath water.

Mr Taylor, who is reported to have very sensitive skin, immediately came out in blotches due to the irritants and allergens contained in the bath bomb.

He was found on the bathroom floor by fellow member John 'Crazyhorse' McCracken, who rubbed Sudocreme on his commander before taking him up to A&E at the Ulster Hospital.

The bombing was condemned by local MLA Barry Mellon who said, 'I am disgusted that a man has broken out in a rash this morning as a result of a despicable and cowardly bath-bombing'.

'Yet again we see the total contempt for a relaxing soak in the tub from some quarters of our society'.

Speaking from his bedside in the Specialist Splish-Splash Unit of the Ulster Hospital, Mr Taylor told us, 'I was lyin there mindin' my own business when suddenly my nostrils were filled with a dreamy scent'.

'Even though the Tunisian neroli lifted my mood and the jasmine and tonka transported me to a floral paradise which I didn't want to leave, I've been left head-to-toe in this rash'.

Asked if it's put him off bathing again, Taylor said, 'No way. I'll still be having a bath every month whether I need one or not'.

Shots at house in East Belfast

Three people were left seriously steaming after rounds of shots were fired down their necks at a house in East Belfast overnight.

Neighbours raised the alarm when they heard multiple shots being 'necked like fuck' followed by some dreadful singing.

One eyewitness reported hearing Flex-Flex-Super-Flex on loop for three and half hours, which was occasionally perforated by cries of 'Yeeeooo'.

Officers responded to the call within hours of finishing a Dominos. When they entered the property they discovered several discarded shot glasses on the floor.

A man and two women woke up in the property this morning and were left badly shaking. The man is being treated for Aftershock.

Damage was caused to the front door, their livers and career prospects.

Responding officers gave the victims Sukie and sausage rolls. It remains unclear whether or not they'll be at work tomorrow.

It's not the first time the home has been targeted after it was pelted with Jaeger Bombs only two weeks ago.

The occupants managed to avoid serious injury on that occasion when a taxi driver brought them a McDonald's breakfast and twenty Regal Kingsize.

Police are appealing to anyone with information to wait until tomorrow as they're having a FIFA tournament at the station tonight.

Parents anguish as gay son comes out as DUP voter

A family from East Belfast have revealed their torment after their rampantly homosexual son revealed that he was a closet DUP voter.

Flight attendant Julian Thompson made the shocking admission to his parents after years of keeping his true political views a secret.

'I'm gutted', confessed his father Jim. 'Bringing home stray cock at all hours of the night I could deal with but a DUP voter? I feel sick just thinking about it'.

His mother revealed that she hasn't been at work since their son dropped the bombshell.

'How can I go in and face anyone when they all know our Julian's an Arelene supporter? He's my heart broke', she sobbed.

Julian, 23, decided to come out on his own because he was threatened with being outed by a neighbour who saw him talking to Gavin Robinson outside his local polling station.

'I think the time has come to be honest and tell everyone that I am a supporter of the Democratic Unionist Party', said the 23-year-old.

'I tried voting for other parties to please my parents but I was living a lie. It feels like a weight off', he added.

The Ryanair employee then took to Facebook to announce the news. 'Fair play to you Jules, we always sorta knew anyway', wrote school friend Daniel Lions.

Gerry Adams launches new range of 'fidget Shinners'

Comedian Gerry Adams is launching a stress-relieving toy for top Republicans who are struggling with the demands of liberating Ireland from British tyranny, it has emerged.

The West Belfast man claims the toy will help those within the Republican movement who may have trouble 'focusing on their objective of 32 county sovereignty'.

Adams is currently on the lookout for a multinational toy company that would be prepared to distribute the new gadget.

'Ehhh, I would like to engage in constructive dialogue with all parties who would be willing to distribute my 'Fidget Shinners', said the bearded one.

However, the DUP, backed by the British government, claim that they will block any attempts by the Sinn Fein president to launch his toy.

The Unionist reaction is in large part down to Sinn Fein objections to a proposed Orange Order revamp of the popular child's toy, LOL Dolls'.

'If we can't have our 'Loyal Orange Order Dolls' in time for the

Twelfth, then Gerry's not getting his fuckin' 'Fidget Shinners' either', said Arlene Foster.

Adams took to social media to vent his frustration. 'Typical Huns, fuckin' kill the craic as usual. However, I would also like to take this opportunity to appeal for calm amongst young Fidgeters – despite this latest example of blatant discrimination'.

However, since the row, Mr Adams has denied ever making a Fidget Shinner.

Politicians Starting to Pretend to Give a Fuck About You

With a little over two weeks before the latest futile Assembly election, politicians across the province are reluctantly mingling with voters and pretending to care about their concerns.

'This election might require a bit more effort' says the DUP's Basil Carrot. 'Normally, I wouldn't set foot inside my own dump of a constituency without some sort of police escort'.

'But according to the polls, which let's face it rarely get any big election result wrong, we're in danger of losing a few votes'.

'Usually, we just put a poster on every lamp post and bung a load of shite through the letterbox. However, on this occasion it would appear that I'm actually going to have to engage some of these filthy peasants by knocking their small non-double-glazed doors'.

Alliance MLA Rodney Jollynice has been trying to attract some new voters by posting his party's slogan on his Facebook account in various regional dialects.

When quizzed about whether or not this was just a shameless last minute ploy to gain a few votes from sections of the community they generally don't give a fuck about, Rodney told us, 'Absolutely'.

'We know we're pissing in the wind with this one but we're desperate. Gaelic, Ulster Scots, fuck I'd even write Change For Good in Klingon if I thought there was enough of them on the electoral register'.

LGBT campaigner Rhonda Fist claims she'll be voting for Sinn Fein this time round. When asked if she thought the gay community in Northern Ireland were being exploited and used as a pawn by Nationalist parties, she said, 'No way. Sinn Fein's entire ethos is based around tolerance'.

Meanwhile, Mike Nesbitt told assembled journalists this morning that he recently discovered he had Polish and Filipino ancestry.

Calls to Ban Election Posters Within 30ft of Schools

PTA groups have rallied together in calling for a ban on election posters outside schools in all constituencies ahead of the assembly election in March.

The move comes after hundreds of primary school children were reportedly having 'bad dreams about the lampposts with the ugly heads'.

The ban is expected to be introduced as a part of Northern Ireland's Public Health Bill, aiming to improve the nation's health, with particular focus on children's wellbeing.

Concerned parent, Susie Muckraker told us, 'Somethin' needs to be done about these posters. They're scaring the shite outta the kids. Our Harry saw Jim Allister's face on a telegraph pole outside his school last year and he's still pissin' the bed at night'.

Sally Rubberneck claims her son has needed specialist counselling after she drove past an election poster belonging to John O'Dowd. She said, 'Our Pearse won't get in the car anymore. He thinks he'll see the scary faces again if he does'.

Pearse, 5, told us, 'We were driving up the road towards the school when suddenly these ugly heads shot quickly past the windows. There was John O'Dowd, Carla Lockhart, Doug Beattie… it was like being on a fuckin' ghost train'.

Meanwhile, one man in East Belfast is hoping that the ban does not come into effect. Dick Tuggington, 41, has been an avid collector of Naomi Long posters since 2003.

Dick explained, 'I love red-heads and I'm not ashamed to admit I've a little thing for Naomi'.

Mr Tuggington then proceeded to show us his little thing and was arrested.

Third Man Dies from Cringe After Watching Arlene Video

The death toll involving the DUP party conference video has risen to three after it emerged another man cringed himself to death.

Russell Patterson, 24, died from 'pure cringe' on his way to the Ulster Hospital after watching a video of the DUP chanting 'Arlene's on fire' at the end of their annual party conference.

Paramedics worked on Mr Patterson for several minutes but they knew they were fighting a losing battle when they discovered his face had exploded from cringing so much.

It's the third such incident to occur since the harrowing footage was released on Saturday evening and doctors have issued a stern warning to those who are thinking of watching the video themselves.

Dr Andre Young of the Specialist Cringing Unit at the Ulster Hospital warned, 'We would appeal to anyone who is thinking of watching this video to stop and think about the consequences'.

'People think they can handle it but this is cringing on a whole new level and the body can't cope. Imagine walking in on your parents bucking while reading through your old Facebook posts on Timehop. Multiply that by 1000 and you're still nowhere near it'.

As well as the three deaths, at least half a dozen others have gouged out their own eyes rendering them permanently blind.

Stevie Charles took his own eyes out with an apple-corer after watching only 6 seconds of the video. He told us, 'I thought taking my eyes out would make it stop. But I can still see it in my head. It was like walking in on your ma taking a shit – on your da'.

A survey revealed that if Arlene was in deed 'on fire' 97% of the gay community wouldn't piss on her.

Court rules Northern Irish woman must give birth to her alien

Northern Irish woman Sigourney McKeever has spoken out after she was told that she must allow a hostile Xenomorph to erupt from her chest, it has emerged.

McKeever (31) became impregnated when a bony finger-like parasitoid known as a 'Facehugger' implanted an embryonic alien into her esophagus in what she claims was a non-consensual manner.

The court argued that McKeever has 'had her face hugged more times than a short person at a funeral' and should therefore be forced to keep her Xenomorph.

It's understood the former Power Loader operator is considering taking the case to the Intergalactic Court of Earthling Rights as the NHS has so far refused to pay for the removal of chest-bursting Xenomorphs.

The DUP, a staunch pro-Alien party, released a statement earlier today which supported the court's ruling on the matter.

'It is our firm belief that everyone has a right to live including highly aggressive endoparasitoid extraterrestrial species. Even Sammy Wilson', said a DUP spokesperson.

In the wake of the decision, former First Minister Arlene Foster emerged from her County Fermanagh home to speak to assembled journalists holding with a fully grown Xenomorph XX121 on the end of a leash.

'Go on, pet her, she won't bite', said the DUP leader, as the snarling beast exposed its pharyngeal jaws.

'There's no such thing as a bad alien – just bad owners. She's great with children', she added.

However, no sooner had the words left Foster's mouth, the Xenomorph broke free from her grasp and leapt upon Jim McDowell from the Sunday World.

'Down Sasha', ordered Arlene - but it was too late. The alien creature's pharyngeal jaw smashed through McDowell's skull like a baby chick hatching from an egg, killing him instantly.

'That's it! Kids, that fucker's going up to the farm in the morning', barked Foster.

4 NORN IRISH SUMMERS

Woman takes photo of her knees to let us all know she's on holiday

A local woman has let everyone on Facebook know she's on holiday by uploading a pic of her knees, it has emerged.

Helen McMelter (38) announced she was jetting off this morning by checking-in at the Lagan Bar in Belfast International Airport and uploading a photograph of a bottle of WKD along with the caption: "And so it begins".

With her social media following on tenterhooks for hours, Helen finally relieved the unbearable suspense by posting a pic of her oiled up knees along with with the phrase: "Living my best life"

Helen was instantly flooded with 'likes' and 'comments' from nosy females and creepy fellas who'd been friend-zoned many years ago.

"Absolutely jel luv. Hope you've a ball", wrote one insincere bastard who couldn't afford a holiday this year.

But not everyone was impressed with Helen's sizzling summer snaps.

Ex-friend Chloe McCreeper, who trawls Facebook hoping to be aggrieved by things, said:

"Look at the state'a thon. Thinks she's some sorta Insta model in that pic and she's legs on her like two frankfurters dipped in chip fat", she snarled.

"And sure she can only afford it cos she got that crisis loan the tramp".

The remainder of Helen's followers are eagerly anticipating the next batch of snaps which are sure to include a bikini selfie and the obligatory one on the balcony before a night out.

Sean Paul to perform 'We Be Burnin' at Shankill Bonfire

Middle-aged Jamaican warbler Sean Paul, AKA 'Shan-a Paaaal', has been booked by local residents to perform at the Shankill bonfire this year, it has emerged.

After wowing the crowds with a mini-set which will include his hits 'We Be Burnin', 'Temperature' and 'Ever Blazin', the rapper will then set fire to the huge wooden structure by lobbing a petrol bomb from the adjacent stage.

It is rumoured that the resident's group first choice was German dance act Scooter but they were already booked to perform at the controversial Chobham Street bonfire.

Sean Paul, real name Dave Brooks, rose to prominence in the early-noughties when he would appear unannounced during other musician's recording sessions and ramble incoherent shite over the top of their singing.

When asked if he'd ever lit a bonfire before, the rapper confidently replied, 'Just gimme the light'.

When asked he if had any concerns about the safety of setting fire to such a tall wooden structure the Jamaican said, 'We be burnin' not concernin' what nobody wanna say'.

The booking has gone down a storm with the younger residents who as a mark of respect have promised that no Jamaican flags will be burnt on the bonfire.

However, not everyone was pleased with the choice of artist for the evening's entertainment.

Local resident Big Lilly Orange, 52, told us, 'You call him wha? Sean Paul? There's no way anyone with a Fenian name like that is getting' up this road let me tell ye'.

NI employers to rename 'July Fornight' as 'Riot Leave'

Westminster is forcing through new legislation which means all Northern Ireland employers must rename 'the July Fortnight' as 'Riot Leave' by 2020, it has emerged.

For many years now, workforces across the province have been given two full weeks holiday in July so that employees can fully participate in violent public disturbances.

Many organisations here appreciate that July provides the perfect conditions for prolonged riotous behaviour with its extended daylight hours and glorious weather.

'We recognise that any sort of structured routine could severely hinder a person's involvement in a running battle with the PSNI or groups of a different religious persuasion', said one local factory owner, Richard Head.

'How could you expect anyone to spend all day lobbing masonry at local law enforcement officers if they're bound by the shackles of a 9-5 shift?', he questioned.

'That's why we give all our staff two full weeks off each year to concentrate on public disorder. A well-rested rioter is a happy rioter', he added.

We caught up with one 50-yr-old menace to society, Chucky Stone, who explained the benefits of a fortnight off work when eager to engage in bitter sectarian street-fighting.

Stone, who was involved in a spot of cross-community brick-throwing at a nearby interface area last night told us: 'Aye, it's good ta get aff work, know whatta mean?', as if he said something so complicated and profound it would require further explanation.

'Means I can launch bricks and petrol bombs at the peelers all night without the fear of any adverse effect on my performance in work the next day due to fatigue'.

'It allows us to spend more time doing the things we love, like lighting big fires or running out of milk at the precise moment a marching band is going past the house'

However, not everyone is happy about the recent influx of holiday hooligans.

Seasoned rioter and long-term sick absentee Claude Mason (49), was less than complimentary about Mr Stones and other fair weather agitators:

'Fuckin' part-timers', he yelled.

Sunburnt Dundonald man thought he was absorbing 'Ulster Volunteer Rays'.

A Dundonald Liberation Army operative is lying in bed covered head-to-toe in natural yoghurt after mistakenly believing that 'U.V. rays' stood for Ulster Volunteer, it has emerged.

As temperatures soared to 30C, Davy 'The Venezuelan' Taylor, 35, decided to take advantage of the glorious weather when he heard that the sun emitted 'U.V. Rays'.

The reputed 'tap mawn' of the DLA thought that if he allowed his skin to absorb the sun's rays then he might attain 'super-powers' which would make him a better freedom fighter.

The 'baitin squad' supremo headed down to the local boney site wearing only a vest and a pair of luminous yellow Nike shorts, equipped with a clinking blue bag.

There he parked his hole on a busted sofa and polished off his cider-based carryout in the baking sun for the better part of five hours.

It wasn't until Taylor nipped home for a bite to eat that he realised he'd been severely sunburnt

'As soon as our Kelly whipped my tap aff you cud see I was pure red raw', winced Taylor while displaying his hideously burnt flesh.

'Obviously a ginger ballix like me shouldn't absorb so many Ulster Volunteer rays'.

His girlfriend Kelly told us, 'I told him this mornin' to put some Factor 50 on. Now luk at him the fat hairy mess. He's half pink and half white. He luks like a fuckin' Drum Stick lally that's been drapped on a barber shap floor'.

She went on, 'I just stick to the fake tawn maself. Fair enough, I might have knuckles and elbows like an Umpa Lumpa's ball-beg on a cold day - but at least am nat rollin' about the bed in pure agony like that labster in the next room'.

With temperatures expected to soar over the coming days, experts are telling people to take the necessary precautions, like avoiding beauty spots filled with gladiator sandal wearing trogs.

Dundonald man literally sweats his balls off

A Dundonald man woke this morning to find that his testicles had dissolved in a puddle of his own sweat, according to reports.

Eunuch Powell, 32, has had terrible difficulty sleeping of late due to the drastic increase in temperatures across Northern Ireland.

The Dundonald man has tried everything from opening a window, to sleeping pure ballick naked.

With temperatures soaring to 25 degrees yesterday, Powell was apprehensive about getting much sleep again.

'By 3am I was sweating like Josef Fritzl on MTV Cribs', said Powell.

He took a Nytol and eventually slipped into a deep sleep but when he woke this morning he was in for a nasty shock.

'My alarm went off at 7am and the first thing I did was slip the aul hand down for my usual morning stock take. But it was all veg and no meat', Powell told us.

'I whipped the quilt back and had a look between my legs. I couldn't believe it, my ballix had melted', added the 32-year-old.

'I started screaming and the Mrs told me to fuck up or I'd wake the kids. When I told her my plums had dissolved and she just laughed in my face', he added.

Nevertheless, Powell went to work as usual, minus his testicles. The Dundonald man admitted it was weird at first but he's sort of gotten used to it now.

'There's less to wash, less to scratch and to be honest she was on my case about getting the snip. Dodged a bullet there', said Powell.

Powell's best mate Big Brick didn't think it would have a huge impact upon his friend's life.

'He lost his ballix the day he met her anyway', claimed Brick.

'Not another fucking BBQ Dad', begs Dundonald child

A 9-year-old boy has pleaded with his father to stop barbecuing meat as the warm weather continues across Northern Ireland.

Big Geordie Foreman, 47, purchased a Weber Genesis II gas barbecue from Homebase last summer hoping to impress friends and family with his cooking prowess in the garden.

Unfortunately, last summer season was wetter than a nursing home sofa after a Daniel O'Donnell televised special and Big Geordie never even got his Weber out of the box.

But the 47-year-old father-of-two has more than compensated for last year's washout by barbecuing every night for the past week.

However, not everyone is happy about the situation, namely, Geordie's 9-year-old son, Ash.

'I fed up to fuck looking at BBQs', moaned Ash.

'Once or twice is ok. But every night that ball-beg's been out there in his novelty apron swinging those tongs about'.

'And why do we need to cook meat over a fire like a street-person when there's a perfectly good kitchen in there with all the necessary amenities to prepare a non-life-threatening meal?', quizzed Ash, while squinting in the sun.

But Big Geordie's BBQ obsession goes deeper than simply cooking outside.

'I can't get it up, I think the wife's leaving me and even the kids don't respect me anymore', said Geordie while turning over a Chinese chicken wing.

'This BBQ represents the last remaining shred of my masculinity - and now, the bastards are trying to take it away as well', he sobbed into an Avengers napkin.

Windowsill becoming insect graveyard

The windowsill of a three bedroom semi in Dundonald is turning into some kind of necropolis for insects, it has emerged.

As relieved occupants can finally open their windows and doors without the risk of flooding or the onset of hypothermia, homes across the province have been infested with winged beasts.

After spending the eight month long Northern Irish winter sleeping in cracks and crannies, flies, wasps, bees and a host of other annoying little pricks are back to ruin everyone's happiness.

Despite finding their way into your home with the greatest of ease, the buzzing little bastards find it almost impossible to leave again.

Whether they perish from exhaustion or a serious head trauma after repeated failed attempts to fly through a solid glass pane, the pests will invariably die a slow and agonising death on the ledge beneath your window.

The result of which leaves your windowsill looking like some sort of garden of remembrance for every species of airborne nuisance.

We caught up with 25-day-old Bee, Honey Bumble, who'd just attended the funeral of her cousin, Buzz, after he'd died on the windowsill of the three bedroom semi.

'It was a beautiful service', wept Honey.

'I bumped into a lot of old friends there who were attending other funerals. In fairness, it was like a mass grave down there', she added.

Three-week-old blue bottle, Martin McFly, was rotating 360 degrees on the windowsill having suffered a serious head wound after mistaking the a glass panel for the open sky.

He said, 'Would someone please just show me the way outta here?'.

'It's not bad enough some mill-beg's been swinging a slipper at me for about fifteen minutes. Now I've gone and split my fuckin' head clean open on this window'.

'And another thing… Oh shit… look out!!!', squealed Martin as a pink fluffy size four Primark slipper crushed him to death.

PSNI reveal new 'anti-debegging' trousers

The PSNI today unveiled their new 'anti-de-begging' trousers as they step up their efforts to combat the brutal punishment administered by the Dundonald Liberation Army (DLA).

Officers demonstrated in front of the assembled media how the new trousers worked by engaging in a tug-of-war with a group of men who are free from the shackles of employment.

An inebriated rotund skinhead volunteered to participate in the experiment and was placed inside the super-keks.

Despite the best efforts of both the police and the stay-at-home-sons, neither side was able to 'de-beg' the test subject.

For years, the Dundonald Liberation Army has used 'de-begging' as a punishment to regulate and curb anti-social behaviour in the neighbourhoods they control.

A recent study compiled by Dundonald Looniversity has shown that the amount of 'de-beggings' has risen by 37% in the past year.

'Despite not boasting a single athlete, most Dundonald inhabitants wear tracksuits, mainly XXL', said Officer Goodfellow.

'While they may be comfortable, they're also very susceptible to a vicious de-begging'.

'With these new anti-de-begging trousers, the people of Dundonald can go about their everyday lives, without the fear of having their keks yanked down to their ankles', added officer Goodfellow.

The move comes after yet another victim was left with injuries described as 'social life changing'.

Several men entered a house on Cherryhill Road at about 19:20 GMT on Monday evening.

A 20-year-old man was taken from the property at water pistol point and dragged up a nearby alley where he was savagely de-begged.

The victim was found with his bags round his ankles several hours later by a woman who was taking her Alsatian for a shite.

Woodvale to host 2018 'squirt-a-Prod' championships

Woodvale has fought off stiff competition from the Crumlin Road and the Shankill Road to host this summer's prestigious 'Squirt-a-Prod' Championships in Belfast.

With help from hometown heroes like the Woodvale Defence Association, the scenic Belfast district aggressively lobbied to host the games.

The announcement was greeted with cries of 'yeeoo' from inhabitants as a drove of pigeons spray-painted red, white & blue were released into the morning sky.

The annual PSNI event draws thousands of spectators onto the streets and is beamed around the globe to millions of viewers.

The 'SAP' Championships sees members of the PSNI riot squad blast inebriated bare-bellied men across great distances using a powerful water cannon.

These fire jets of water at various speeds, depending on the aggressiveness and girth of the drunken Prod mounting PSNI landrovers

Last year, Officer Goodfellow of the PSNI set a new world record when he sent a 15-stone man in Rangers shorts skidding a distance of 45ft on his arse.

'I remember the gentleman fondly', recalls officer Goodfellow.

'He hopped up onto a Landrover bonnet clutching a tin of Tennents in each hand whilst doing the bouncy'.

'As soon as the water skelpt him across his hairy moobs, I knew it was a world record contending effort'.

This year's event is expected to draw even more contestants onto the streets as they hope to become the latest in a long line of squirted Prods.

Former record-holder and ever-present participant in the championships, Bap McBride, told us, 'It's quare craic so it is. I've been fortunate enough to be squirted every year – except 2014 – I was in Alacante on a feg-run that year'.

The opening ceremony for this year's games will take place on July 1st where music will be provided by Dutch dance-pop act Artmesia who will be performing their club-classic 'Bits & Pieces'.

Northern Ireland calendar upgrades to five seasons to include 'Marching'

Northern Ireland has decided to amend its calendar-based seasons to include 'Marching', it has been revealed.

The region normally adhered to the standard four divisions of the year, including Spring, Summer, Autumn and Winter, which result from the earth's changing position with regard to the sun.

However, after careful consideration, the decision was taken to increase the amount of seasons to five in order to incorporate the nation's favourite hobby.

'People in other countries can usually tell which season they're in by changes in weather patterns and daylight hours. However, because Northern Ireland is ball-freezing and wet twelve months of the year, this can prove tricky', said ginger sex-god Barra Best.

'By officially recognising Marching Season as a part of the Northern Irish calendar, people will know that it's somewhere between Spring and Summer', added the strawberry blonde lothario.

'While winter is synonymous with snow and summer with sun, marching season will be identifiable with traffic jams and violent clashes at interface areas', he added.

All office stationary, calendars and school syllabuses have been updated to include the new season.

'I just had a wee flick through my new calendar' said civil servant Basil Sloth.

'In spring there's a picture of a little lamb frolicking in a field. In autumn it's a forest floor covered in red and yellow leaves. And in marching there's an angry mob being dispersed by a police water cannon. Beautiful'.

However, not everyone welcomed the move. Concerned president of the Four Seasons hotel Ltd, Allen Smith, complained, 'This is an outrage! I was hoping to open a hotel in Belfast but now they have bloody five seasons. A person should be able to go about their normal daily lives without being subjected to such discrimination'.

Man dragged kicking and screaming against his will onto Ryanair flight

The world was united in anger today after footage emerged of a man being dragged kicking and screaming onto a Ryanair flight.

The video posted to social media shows a man being violently trailed on board an empty Irish low-cost airliner whilst crying out for his mother.

CCTV footage leaked from Belfast International Airport shows security personnel snatch the man from inside the terminal after he declined a one thousand euro bribe to fly with the airline.

It's the latest in a series of dastardly schemes employed by Ryanair as they desperately seek anyone of sound mind to use their service.

'My God, what are you doing? This is evil', one woman cries as she watches the man being dragged past her feet.

Big Tina McCourt, who posted a video of the encounter to Facebook, wrote that airline staff were looking for one volunteer to board the plane free of charge.

But as they struggled to find anyone willing, the staff began to offer incentives including one thousand euros in cash and a two week stay in CEO Michael O'Leary's home.

'No matter what they offered, people refused to voluntarily board the plane. People all around me were burning their passports and some were even claiming to have bombs in their luggage', added Mrs McCourt.

A spokesperson for the company said, 'We can confirm there was an incident today involving one of our planes. However, we charge you less for a flight to London than a taxi would from Belfast to Newtownards, so lick them'.

In other news, the airline today announced that all customers with at least one divorce under their belt will be hit with an additional 'baggage' charge.

5 BAKEBOOK

Investigation launched after holidaymakers skip Lagan Bar Facebook check-in

An investigation is underway at Belfast International Airport after a couple of holidaymakers failed to check themselves in at the Lagan Bar using Facebook.

The couple (who cannot be named for legal reasons) were taken to an on-site custody suite by airport security staff and questioned about the incident.

One eyewitness in the Lagan Bar described the moment the pair sat down with their drinks about 7.30am this morning.

'Everything seemed perfectly normal at first', described the eyewitness.

'They went to the bar and bought their drinks. But whenever they sat down, that's when things got strange'.

'Instead of whipping out their smartphones and taking photos of the drinks, they just drank them'.

'Then they started talking to one another instead of aimlessly scrolling up and down their phones'.

'It was almost as if the entire trip wasn't for everyone's benefit and they actually enjoyed each other's company?'.

'I kept waiting on a phone coming out but nothing. No photos of the drinks, no Facebook check-ins nor a caption reading 'And so it begins' with accompanying aeroplane emoji - fuck all', added the eyewitness.

A spokesperson for the airport confirmed that a couple were helping officials with their enquiries after an incident this morning.

As news of the incident broke, other holidaymakers took to social media to express their outrage.

'How the fuck are we supposed to know when someone's holiday begins unless they check-in on Facebook at the Lagan Bar. This will lead to chaos', Tweeted one disgruntled flyer.

'No Lagan Bar check-in? What next? No photos on the balcony before a night out? Total madness. I blame Brexit', Tweeted another.

Local woman reactivates her Facebook account after three day hiatus

A Dundonald woman abruptly ended her self-imposed Facebook ban after three days and then conceded, 'Well, that lasted long'.

Shelly 'Loyal', 28, made the announcement 72 hellish hours after of being unable to pry on the lives of people she knows but can no longer stand.

This constituted an embarrassing U-turn for Shelly after she posted a withering assessment of Facebook and everyone who uses it, a few hours before deactivating her account.

In a long-winded expletive ridden rant, Shelly wrote, 'Does anyone know how ya delete this thing for good? Fed up reading about everyone's perfect lives when we all know the f**kin' truth. Half the b**tards on this thing wouldn't even say hello to ya in the street'.

'Don't delete it hun, time for a clear out me thinks', wrote Shelly's friend Nicola 'Scentsy' Jones in a comment under the post. 'Awk, I'll miss your wee rants', wrote another.

Despite her nosy friend's pleas, Shelly followed through with her threat and deactivated her account on Monday night.

Shelly instantly regretted her decision even though she was still able to track her friend's every movements via Instagram, Snapchat and various other media.

Desperate to catch up on all the gossip, Shelly swallowed her pride and reactivated her account.

Later that morning Shelly posted, 'Does anyone have the number to the doctor's surgery?'.

'Google', commented one local raker.

Local melter sets up third new Facebook profile this year

A 24 karat gold 'melter' has gone and set himself up another new Facebook profile, it has emerged.

Hundreds of unsuspecting people woke this morning to a new friend request from local 'balloon-head' Dave McDramagh.

Every six months or so, the 37-year-old deactivates his Facebook account only to re-emerge several weeks later with a new profile under a slightly different pseudonym.

The former Herbal Life Rep, Scentsy Consultant and Crypto Currency Trader has appeared under aliases such as: Davy McD; Dee McDee & DramaDave.

Dave's biannual meltdowns normally conclude with a long-winded Facebook rant claiming 'this is the last you'll hear from me'.

However, after getting everyone's hopes up, Dave reappears several months later with a new Facebook page and a fake inspirational quotation from Tom Hardy.

The reasons for Dave's cyber sabbaticals vary but we caught up with part-time sales assistant and full-time nosy bastard, Leanne Tattler, who used to ride Dave's brother.

'Well ni, let me see. I fink he was being chased by the CSA so he had to delete his old Facebook. Then he was gonna get kneecapped for sending a dick pic to the tap man's daughter so he deleted the one after that', explained Leanne.

'Then he put up a post trying to excuse his heinous behaviour over the past twenty years because he was depressed but no one bought it, so he deleted that one too', she added.

When asked if she'd be deleting Dave's new friend request, Leanne said, 'Are ya mad? How the hell would I get my day in?'.

Man forgets to take his phone to the gym

A man was reduced to tears in a local gym after realising he'd left his phone at home, it has emerged.

Andy Bolic (25) made the grizzly discovery when he tried to take the first of his many workout-related selfies this morning.

The self-proclaimed 'gym freak' would usually post about twenty photos of himself online over the course of normal training session.

These images of Andy flexing in front of a mirror are normally accompanied by some bullshit inspirational quotation he's copied and pasted from the ramblings of some other bell-end who thinks that lifting weights makes him a modern day Plato.

'I'd just ingested a large energy drink and was slipping into 'beast mode' when I realised I'd forgotten my iPhone', recalled Andy.

'I mean, what's the point of even going to the gym if you can't let everyone on Facebook know about it?', he sobbed.

'I had it all planned it out', he explained.

'My first pic was gonna be me flexing my bicep while inexplicably wearing an over-sized flat-peaked baseball cap indoors'.

'Then I'd attach a caption to it like 'you only have one body, make sure you take care of it', which is ironic because I've been injecting a dangerous cocktail of growth hormones I've prescribed off the internet into my buttocks', he added.

Meanwhile, fellow 18-stone gym-goer Jeremy Sloth puts Andy's incredible physique simply down to steroids.

'I'd be his shape to if I took steroids', said Jeremy while collecting a share bag of Haribo from the reception's vending machine.

Local man tells internet about his 'inspiring' encounter with a homeless person

A Dundonald man who posted a long-winded Facebook status about his inspiring encounter with a homeless person is adamant that he isn't just fishing for likes, it has emerged.

Kyle Goodman, 23, was walking through the town centre when a homeless man made the terrible mistake of asking him for 'spare odds'.

The beleaguered man's request sparked a eureka moment for Kyle who sprang into action.

'If I gave him money he probably would've spent it on something ghastly like booze or a blow job off a heroin addict. So I went and got him a 6-inch Sub and a hot drink instead.', explained Kyle.

'I sat down beside him for a chat and tried to establish – in a totally unpatronizing way – why he was lying in the street caked in his own shite'.

'While he was describing how the bank sold him a 125% mortgage he couldn't afford then seized his home, I decided to share his story without his consent on the internet', Kyle added.

'So I whipped out my iPhone X and took a selfie with him. The sun must've been in his eyes or something cos he was putting his hand across his face'.

The homeless man, Frank Hobo (42), although very grateful for the six inch Meatball Marinara, had an inkling he'd end up in a longwinded Facebook post.

'While I was telling Kyle about the perils of sub-prime lending, I could tell his mind was elsewhere'.

'It was almost as if he was writing that Facebook post in his head instead of listening to my story', said Frank.

'If I was a suspicious fella, I'd say Kyle was using me a pawn in some despicable scheme to make himself look like a hero and maybe get his hole out of it'.

'But hey, at least I don't have to wank someone off for grub today'.

Man takes his kids to soft play area to spend quality time with his phone

A local man has taken his kids to a soft-play area in order to spend some quality time with his smartphone, it has emerged.

Sonny Ericson (36), who works long hours during the week, has become increasingly concerned that he might be neglecting his phone.

The father-of-three explained:

"I feel so guilty. I spend so much time working and running after the kids my phone barely gets a look in these days".

"It's my first weekend off in six weeks. So I thought I'd take Jake, Sophie and eh, the other one, to this new idiot-proofed industrial unit called Happy World".

"The coffee's decent; it has free Wifi; oh, and the kids will fuck off and leave me alone for two hours".

"Daddy, can I have a drink?', 'Daddy, I need the toilet', 'Daddy, I can't eat that I'm allergic' – they're so bloody demanding".

"But taking them to a soft-play area means I can do the things which really matter".

"Like have a row in the comments section of a Facebook post about a

Genderbread Person or sharing graphic sexual videos in a WhatsApp group".

Sonny's son Jake (8), is hoping this bonding session with the phone will ease his father's suffering.

"It's hard to watch him in so much pain. I know how much he cares about that phone".

"I have to say 'Dad' five times before he'll lift his head but if he hears an SMS alert he's bounding over armchairs like Colin Jackson to find it".

'Wide Awake Club' a group of nosy bastards afraid of missing something

A ground breaking new study has revealed that 97% of members of the 'wide awake club' are in fact just 'nosy bastards afraid of missing something'.

Boffins at the Dundonald Institute of Government Funded Ridiculous Studies ran rigorous tests on one hundred subjects who claim to be members of a nocturnal online society.

The results showed nearly all of these people would find it much easier to sleep if they'd put their smartphone in a drawer and stopped staring at a bright glowing screen.

'We unearthed a direct correlation between a patient's inability to sleep and excessive creeping on Facebook', said Dr Andre Young

'The fact these ballbags are willingly forgoing sleep in order to pry on the lives of others means any claims of insomnia are indeed bogus', he added.

Treasurer of the 'Wide Awake Club', Helen McMelter, said, 'As soon as my head hits the pilla', my brain goes haywire. I'm not sure whether it's a lack of any mental or physical exertion during the day or if it's a genuine sleeping disorder. Hopefully these tests get 'til the bottom of it'.

'Last night I sat up til 4.30am sending screen grabs of a Facebook row to my mate Shazzy that she couldn't see cos the wee girl had blocked her. It was terrible. I ended up lying in til lunchtime today', she explained.

When asked if he'd any advice for others out there who are thinking of joining the 'Wide Awake Club', Dr Young said, 'Yes. Turn your phone off and close your fucking eyes'.

Local woman celebrates 70yrs of NHS with Facebook A&E check-in

A Dundonald woman is celebrating the 70th anniversary of the National Health Service by making her weekly trip to the local A&E department, it has emerged.

Helen McMelter arrived a short while ago in a taxi sporting a pink dressing down and clutching a floral patterned soap bag.

The 31-year-old Scentsy Consultant suffers from an indeterminable condition that flares up on a weekly basis which leaves her no other option than to head straight to A&E.

After getting herself a tin of Red Bull and King Size Snickers from the vending machine, Helen took her usual seat and whipped out her new Galaxy S7 she bought on the Woodvale Buy & Sell Facebook page.

'Oh here we go again' she wrote in a vague cryptic post whilst informing everybody on Facebook of her precise location.

It wasn't long before the usual assortment of nosy motherfuckers spotted Helen's update and began to offer their opinions.

First to comment under the post was Helen's cousin, Shelly who demanded to know, 'What's wrong nii??'.

'Awk hun, you're not having a good run of it at all lately. Let me know if ya need anything dropped up', typed another local busybody, Amber.

'Bloody joke luv. You'd think they'd have got this sorted by now', wrote her friend Kelly, who wouldn't have the medical experience to squeeze a pimple.

After leaving her Facebook audience on tenterhooks for a couple hours,

Helen finally delivered a much anticipated update on her situation:

'Just waiting on the big Doc coming to see me nii. Fingers crossed they finally find out what's wrong this time'.

After a careful examination, Dr Steph O'Scope of the Specialist Drama Unit concluded:

'Helen appears to be suffering from a chronic case of attention seeking hypochondriac bastard's disease'.

'We've put her on a lifetime course of anti-neurotics'.

Tullycarnet family's ordeal after power cut leaves them without WiFi for four hours

A family in Tullycarnet have spoken about their ordeal after a power cut left them without Wifi for almost four hours today.

Emergency services were alerted to the situation at 11.30am this morning after father-of-two Tony Erickson (43), dialled 999 and signalled for help.

Crews arrived on the scene a few minutes later and found the family-of-four in an 'extremely distressed' state and begging for internet access.

They were immediately wrapped in blankets and whisked away to a local café which provides free Wifi for customers.

'I'm just relieved our nightmare is finally over', wept Mr Erickson whilst checking his Bet365 app.

'At first we all thought the hub was on the blink again. So I told our Nathan to turn it off and on', he explained.

'But after a few unsuccessful attempts to sign back in I knew we were all fucked'.

His wife Sylvia describes the harrowing moment the family realised there was no Wifi.

'I was in the middle of a bidding war for a tumble dryer with some hoor on the Woodvale Buy & Sell Facebook page when suddenly it crashed', she explained.

'I guldered at Tony to get off his hole and fix the internet but he said the electric was off. That's when I knew we'd have to tell the kids'.

Their 14-year-old son Nathan took the news the hardest and ran off down the street with his iPhone in the air to see if he could pick up someone else's signal but to no avail.

Back in the café, medical professionals were in the process of teaching Nathan to communicate verbally again after he'd spent the past two years conversing only in Gifs and emojis.

'It's hard seeing your son this way', said Tony.

'He wasn't able to watch Pornhub for over four hours'.

'I tried showing him a few of my old Playboy mags but when I told him it didn't have Mia Khalifa section as she was probably only a foetus when it was published, he lashed out'.

If anyone has been affected by today's power cut, please don't dial 101 and report it to the PSNI like the person who reported yesterday that a sun bed shop had closed down but still owed them 25 minutes.

All future rape trials to take place on Facebook

All future rape trials in Northern Ireland will take place on Facebook to free up some much needed funds for things like potholes, it has emerged.

A newly established 'NI Court of Bakebook' is set to save the taxpayer around £100m per year according to reports.

The move has been welcomed with many people believing the existing judicial system is tedious and 'outdated'.

'Traditional trials were slow as fuck', explained Minister for Justice and Equality, Charles Flanagan.

'The new Court of Bakebook will replace due process with scurrilous accusations and rush to judgements'.

'All future rape claims will be posted straight to Facebook where the public will be invited to leave their damning verdict in the comments section'.

'Anyone with a Facebook account can give evidence. It could be a police officer handling the case, the complainant or just someone on long-term sick with fuck all better to do during the day than trawl through Facebook hoping to be offended'.

'When the public has found some other social media cause to champion, we tally up all the guilty and not guilty comments'.

'And once a verdict has been reached, we then ask the public what the punishment should be. It's usually something fair like a skinning or a burning alive'.

'Any monies saved can be used for more essential things, like changing street names into eight regional dialects or paying MLA's porn movie bills in hotels', he added.

Man arrested for 'It's snowing' Facebook post

A 33-year-old Belfast man was arrested this morning after 'stating the fucking obvious', it has emerged.

Michael Kettley was seized by the PSNI shortly after posting, 'it's snowing', on his Facebook page.

The bloodied man was dragged kicking and screaming into a waiting Landrover where he was given 'a good hiding', according to eyewitnesses.

'We can all see it's fucking snowing', said a PSNI spokeswoman.

'Anyone with half-functioning eyes and windows is fully aware of the tons of frozen crystalline water falling from the skies above'.

'It's not as if we're all wondering what it is and eagerly awaiting his fucking amateur weather report complete with a snowflake emoji'.

'Let this be a warning to any other wanker who's thinking of acting Barra

Best this morning', she added.

Speaking from his cell in Maghaberry, Mr Kettley said, 'This is a breach of my human rights. I'll be taking this to the courts and you can rest assured… hold on, what's that I see through my cell window… is it?... it is… IT'S SNOWING!!!'

Meanwhile evil Mark Zuckerberg spoke of the enormous strain that's been placed upon Facebook's servers as hordes of arseholes post countless photos of the snow.

'We canny hold her, she's gonna blow', said the CEO whilst fanning away the smoke with a wad of $100 bills.

'Time for a clear out me thinks' announces local woman

A Dundonald woman has signalled her intentions to cull her Facebook friends list, it has emerged.

Kelly McMelter (28), made the announcement on her Facebook page shortly after 9am this morning in a post which read:

'Time for a clear out me thinks. Too many people carrying tales back to my ex'. Kelly then concluded the post with three snake emoji's.

The drastic move comes after information was leaked to her ex-boyfriend Wayne and Kelly is adamant there's a mole in the camp.

'I told Wayne's he couldn't have the kids this weekend cos they were sick and he was raging', explained Kelly.

'I was so stressed out by the kid's having the cold that I asked my ma to mind them so I could go to Benedicts'.

'I bumped into this lovely group of fellas from Sandy Row and I posed for a few selfies with them. When I uploaded the photos to the internet, I never imagined for one second that the information might be passed back to my ex and he'd get upset'.

'I know I voluntarily upload every single aspect of my existence onto a public platform which is potentially accessible to millions of people – but

I'm a very private person at the end of the day', she added.

Top of the comments section under the post was Kelly's friend Natalie. Natalie, who spends the majority of her mornings flicking between Kelly's and Wayne's Facebook pages wrote:

'Just right hun. Hope I survive the cull', followed by several praying hands and laughing emoji's.

'When I saw Kelly was deleting people, I almost dropped my phone', explained Natalie.

'I'd be lost if I didn't have her page to stalk all day. I'd probably have to do something like seek daytime employment or concentrate on my own problems'.

Jay Z Blocks Beyoncé on Facebook

Ugly millionaire heartthrob Jay Z has responded to his wife Beyoncé's accusations of cheating by blocking her off Facebook.

Subsequently, the man 'from the streets', who's worth $56m is also said to be 'pure ragin' with himself that he ever recorded a track which claimed he had '99 Problems' but a bitch was not one of them.

Meanwhile, Beyoncé is said to be completely shocked by her husband's infidelities because the 'Big Pimpin' singer came across as 'really respectful' and 'not misogynistic at all' in his rap songs.

The trouble flared between the pair last Saturday when Beyoncé's album Lemonade was released and Jay Z heard her song 'Sorry', which music insiders claim is about Jay Z 'buckin all 'round him'.

In retaliation, Jay Z blocked the 'Crazy in Love' singer off his Facebook and set about organising a night out with the boys that weekend. Beyoncé changed her relationship status to 'single' and was inundated with comments from friends that she hadn't spoken to since before she got married.

Kelly Rowland wrote under the post, 'Keep yer head held high luv. Ppl no the truth now. Karma's a bitch' and then inexplicably finished it off with an emoji of some clapping hands. Michelle Williams, the other one of her mates who no one ever remembers, wrote, 'PM me chick ♥'.

Since then Beyoncé's been out on the piss every night with Kelly and Michelle. The three girls have been posting photographs of themselves in various nightclub toilets and writing captions about how friends are forever, at least until one of them finds a new boyfriend then they'll sever all ties again.

After an unsuccessful night out on the pull, Jay Z returned back to his ma's spare room and sent pictures of his cock to disinterested ex-girlfriends. The following morning he posted a Facebook status about joining the gym and getting ripped for a holiday to Ibiza he hadn't booked yet.

Beyonce then changed all her Facebook posts to 'public' so that all of Jay Z's mates could tell him about how much fun she's having and how she's moved on with her life.

6 LIFESTYLE

East Belfast Avon dealer viciously attacked

A suspected Avon dealer has suffered potentially 'career-changing' injuries after a vicious beating, police have said.

The victim, a renowned make-up pusher, was taken to the Ulster Hospital where he is having a foundation brush surgically removed from his rectum.

Graffiti claiming 'Avon dealers will be shat' was daubed on wall close to where the attack took place.

Police are treating the situation as 'fucking hilarious'.

Mark Anew has been selling his product on the streets of East Belfast for several years despite repeated threats from local paramilitary bosses to stop.

The 39-year-old was spotted going door-to-door around Glenallen Street yesterday evening when he was set upon by a posse of men.

When asked whether he recognised any of his attackers, Mark responded: 'Na, they were wearing face-masks – and I'm not talking about a Clearskin facial either'.

There have been rumours that Anew's own teenage sons, Bazza and Spanker may have been involved in the attack.

The brothers have been subjected to cruel taunts from classmates about their father being an Avon dealer and sources believe they may have even instigated the assault.

'We can't even show our faces in public for the shame', confessed Spanker.

'Why can't he just sell drugs like everyone else's Da?', sobbed Bazza.

Local man almost suffocates underneath wife's plastic bag collection

A Dundonald man almost suffocated this morning when he opened a kitchen cupboard and was trapped underneath an avalanche of plastic bags his wife had been hoarding.

Big Geordie Morrisons (47) also suffered a broken fibula when he was 'almost crushed to death' by a giant bag full of bags which rolled over the top of him.

'I was looking for the Fairy-up liquid cos I'd oil on my hands. So I opens the cupboard under the sink and the next fing it's like the boulder scene from Indiana Jones', explained Geordie.

'This massive ball of plastic rolled over my legs and I was trapped underneath it. I lay on the kitchen floor for three hours crying for help til she came back from Slimming World', he moaned.

His wife, Lydia (43), was forced to buy another half dozen reusable shopping bags yesterday after forgetting to bring hers to the supermarket for 352nd time in a row.

'I've a head like a sieve', admitted Lydia.

'I have about two thousand bags for life inside a bag for life under the sink'.

'As soon as I got to the til, yer woman asked me if I'd like a wee bag.

That's when it dawned on me I'd need to buy another six or seven', she chuckled.

Her husband Geordie was less amused by the incident.

'That's me on the statutory sick and Christmas fucked. But sure she got slimmer of the week. Whoopdy fuckin' doo', he added.

Gin replaces craft beer as the No.1 alcoholic beverage for pretentious wankers.

Boffins today announced that following on from 2013's craft beer explosion, gin has become the No.1 alcoholic beverage for pretentious wankers.

Dr Steph O'Scope who carried out the research explained, 'A simple scroll through one's social media platforms on a Friday night will reveal countless photographs of people clutching unnecessarily large gin glasses containing needlessly expensive gin, tonic, ice and lime'.

'Of course populist muck such as Gordons is out the window. The more obscure and expensive the brand the better. Then the drinker can regale us all with their insurmountable knowledge of the weird tasting spirit', she added.

The results showed that currently 87% of people between the ages of 12 and 75 drink an average of six litres of gin per day.

However, researchers predict that figure will rise to 99.7% by 2021 with pompous gins expected to solve drought issues in Central and East Africa.

'We've found that replacing water with gin reduces the risk of a long life expectancy and saves a fortune in foreign aid', explained Sally Goodheart of the Red Cross.

'We've tested out the model in Togo, Uganda, Bangladesh, Mozambique and North Belfast since 2014 with great success', she added.

However, not everyone is conforming to the widespread gin-drinkery.

Big 'Dinger' Bell from East Belfast told us he doesn't see the fascination.

'It's fuckin' ratten', barked Mr Bell.

'Standing there swirling their silly big glass thinking they are something'.

'It's made outta spuds and berries and gets ya pished. Give me twenty tins of cheap Danish lager any day'.

Pamela Ballantine dyes, aged 60

Revered Northern Irish television presenter Pamela Ballantine has dyed at her home in Belfast, it has emerged.

The UTV stalwart was last seen leaving Tescos Knocknagoney with a box of Clairol's Nice n' Easy around 9pm last night.

The usually silver-haired presenter was found slumped over a sink at her home by a friend.

She confirmed to reporters outside the presenter's home that Pamela was alone when she dyed.

The reason why the 60-year-old decided to dye are still unclear but an investigation will be carried out shortly.

The former Downtown Radio host has a broadcasting career spanning almost 30-years.

Friends and former colleagues have paid tribute to Pamela in the wake of the shocking news.

Legendary Northern Irish presenter Jackie Fullerton was one of the first to react.

Jackie Tweeted: 'Absolutely gobsmacked at the news'.

'I can't believe Pamela dyed so young. I'm 75 and I still haven't dyed yet'.

Fellow broadcaster and compatriot Eamon Holmes was reportedly 'stunned' when informed that Pamela had dyed.

The Sky News presenter Tweeted: 'Still in shock. Pamela was just one of those people you never thought would dye'.

Northern Irish golfing hero Darren Clarke is still coming to terms with news.

He said, 'I can't believe it. Of all the people I thought would dye, Pamela certainly wasn't one of them'.

The shocking news will come as a major blow to UTV who were in talks with Ballantine regarding a new documentary about silver-headed Northern Irish sex-symbols entitled, '50 Shades of Grey-Haired Rides.

Culchie wearing skinny jeans found badly beaten

A young Tyrone farmer was found badly beaten after it emerged he purchased a pair of skinny jeans, according to reports.

Garth Carter was set upon by a gang of up to eight people after he returned from a shopping trip to 'the big smoke', during which he purchased jeans which were not regulation boot-cut.

Garth's battered body was stumbled upon by dog-walkers who immediately rang an ambulance.

The 24-year-old is recovering in the Royal Victoria Hospital where his condition is said to be 'Wile bad, hi'.

'I hear them townie weemen like a fella in a pair of those skinny numbers. So, I thought I'd get meself a pair for the dancing that night', explained Garth.

'But when I arrived back in Tyrone I was approached by a group of lads with GAA shirts on and they asked to see inside the bag, hi'.

'When they saw the 'super skinny' label on the jeans I took a whack across the teeth with a hurley stick'.

'Then they set upon me like a pack of wolves. I could hear them shouting, 'how the fuck are they gonna roll down over your boots?, he sobbed.

A local gang, calling themselves 'Culchies Upholding Normal Traditions' or 'C.U.N.T.S', have claimed responsibility for the attack.

'Garth knows the dress code: check shirt, boot-cut jeans and brown square-toed loafters', said a spokesperson for the group.

'It's imperative we uphold the Culchie way of life. If we let one Ginny-ann prance about here in skinny jeans, the next thing you know lads won't be driving the back roads from the age of 12 or listening to Happy Hardcore in their tractors'.

Local woman looking forward to getting her jammies on and lighting a Jo Malone candle later

A Dundonald woman wants to put her pyjamas on before burning an overpriced scented candle tonight, it has emerged.

Helen McMelter announced the news in a Facebook post shortly after 10am this morning which read:

'Looking forward to getting home the night, sticking my new jammies on and lighting my Pomegranate Noir Home Jo Malone Candle. Bliss'.

Helen is just one of many people these days who are paying upwards £50 for a lump of smelly wax in a jar.

'Yankee Candles are out the fuckin' windy', explained Helen.

'I wouldn't insult my nostrils with any of that cheap shite', she added.

Upon returning home that night, Helen lit her new candle with a wooden splint and then spent the next 45 minutes trying to capture the perfect Insta snap of the fragranced block of wax.

Once she'd acquired the right photo, Helen posted it online along with a dozen wanky hashtag slogans about cosy winter nights in with her candle.

The Jo Malone candle is often bought in conjunction with crushed-velvet furniture and pink gin.

Parents rejoice as two month hell ends

Parents across Northern Ireland are today celebrating the end of a two month nightmare commonly referred to as the 'Summer Holidays'.

There were high-fives among pyjama-clad women at school gates across the country this morning, after they frogmarched their spawn into the care of trained professionals.

The beleaguered parents were overheard discussing the various ways they planned to spend the next few blissful child-free hours.

Mother of two, Danielle Freeman said, 'Thank f**k it's over. Any school holidays longer Obviously somebody without any kids came up with the idea of two months off for summer'.

'I left the wee bastards at the gates about 8.55am then headed straight for the Winemark. I'm gonna lie on my hole, watch Diagnosis Murder and polish off this crate of West Coast Cooler Rose'.

Her husband Morgan spent the past two months pretending to be Darth Vader while having plastic sword fights with their five-year-old son Toby.

He told us, 'I think I've developed a curvature of the spine from stooping down so much'.

'I don't think I could've taken one more afternoon of that wee ballix putting on a fake American accent and whacking me on the knuckles'.

'I think I'm gonna hit the Shebeen and do some shots. The world's my oyster', he added.

Their 7-year-old son Harry was equally as relieved to be returning to school.

He said, 'There are only so many trips to a soft-play area full of rough council estate children one can stomach'.

'I dunno what they're so relieved about anyway? They may as well have handed custody over to the Xbox for the holidays'.

'You should've seen my mother this morning sobbing and waving at me like I was leaving for a tour of Iraq. She wasn't getting on like that when she going to Alibi on Saturday night'.

Nine motorists bored to death in Titanic Quarter bus lane tailbacks

The death toll continues to rise after a ninth motorist died from boredom whilst stuck in traffic congestion on the Queen's Road.

It brings the total number of commuters who've perished in their vehicles to fifty since the introduction of the new bus lanes around Belfast.

The Department for Infrastructure Communications Service (or DICS for short), said the delays had been 'greater than we never bothered our holes to anticipate'.

A spokesperson said that white lily wreaths shaped like the Glider logo had been sent to the victim's families.

The PSNI confirmed four of the deceased had bashed their brains out on their steering wheels when their phone batteries died and they were forced to listen to Cool FM.

The new road layout is to accommodate Belfast's new 'Bendy-Bus' system which has spectacularly failed in every other major city in the United Kingdom.

In response to spate of boredom related fatalities, the Department for Infrastructure said it would revise traffic light timings in the area.

Mr P. S. Takker, who works in Belfast's Traffic Control room told us:

'It's great to see them get their wee hopes up when the light turns green'.

'Then, less than a nanosecond later, we switch it to amber again. The devastation on their faces is plain to see'.

With even more congestion anticipated this evening , sanctimonious do-gooders will be providing food rations and warm clothing to people stuck on the Sydenham and Queen's Road.

Some motorists finally emerged from their vehicles this morning highly disorientated and unaware exactly how long in the traffic jams.

One women said she experienced 'the change of life' while trapped inside her car while other people underwent even greater metamorphose, according to the PSNI.

'An 11-year-old school boy left the Titanic Quarter car park at 4.55pm. By the time he reached the bottom of the Queen's Road his voice had broken and he'd grown a beard', confirmed Constable Goodfellow.

'And when he finally reached his destination he had three kids and a mortgage'.

The situation is even more dire on the Newtownards Road where the people have been stuck in traffic so long they're still driving Morris Minors and Ford Anglias.

Belfast parents quietly hoping daughter fails A- levels

A couple from East Belfast who promised their daughter money for every passing grade she achieved in her A-Levels, are secretly hoping that she fails every exam she sat.

Jim and Maureen Crook from Ballyhackamore told their daughter Megan she'd get £100 for a C, £250 for a B and £500 for an A.

'Like her da, she's thick as fuck', said Maureen. 'So, the likelihood of her getting any money off us at all is slim'.

'But here we are, all nervously huddled together in the front hall beside the letterbox. One or two surprise results could see us down a f**king fortune'.

'With any luck she'll get straight Us', said father Jim.

'Any money she gets for good results will be coming straight out my kitty for gear and hookers on the next Rangers trip'.

But Megan isn't overly bothered about what grades she gets as she believes her future is already mapped out.

'Jim and Maureen are broke. So, it's not as if they can pull any strings and set me up in a cushy number in some well-paid job', explained Megan.

'Unfortunately, a combination of things I have zero control over has already predetermined the rest of my life'.

'I'm just gonna sponge off these two for as long as I can before they kick me out or I find myself an ageing millionaire with a bad heart'.

'A-Levels are a pile of pointless shite anyway'.

'Google, auto-correct and calculators have rendered most syllabuses useless'.

'I bet I can go through the rest of my life without ever having to use long-division or asking someone where the nearest train station is in French', he added.

Man dies from hangover in Holywood Exchange IKEA

A man has died from a hangover in the Holywood Exchange branch of IKEA, it has emerged.

36-year-old Stevie McGreedy's body was discovered by staff curled up in the foetal position on a HÖVÅG pocket sprung mattress.

Paramedics arrived on the scene within minutes where he was pronounced dead.

The death has prompted calls from men's rights groups for new laws which prohibits women from dragging their hungover spouses around the chain of notorious Swedish gulags.

For years, men have been forced against their will to walk around the Scandinavian death-camps whilst suffering from acute alcohol withdrawal.

The evil females often exact revenge on a male partner for having enjoyed himself the previous evening by making him wade through flat-pack furniture the next day.

Another Belfast man, Toby Jug, says he almost died in the same IKEA store just last month.

The 42-year-old was found on a yellow fabric KNOPPARP sofa by staff who described Mr Jug as 'fucking dying'.

They managed to stop Toby's condition from deteriorating by feeding him Sprite and Swedish meatballs from the cafeteria.

'I'd a full crate of Coors the night before', recalled Toby.

'The next morning she said, 'You may get your lazy drunken hole up, we're going to IKEA'.

'Whoever designed that place is clearly a sadist. It's like some giant evil board game'.

'Once you enter, you've no choice other than to walk around the whole warehouse to get back out again'.

Recalling the incident, Toby's wife Liz remarked:

'Aye they can try to stop us taking them to IKEA but no one said anything about Primark, did they nai?'.

Man reveals ordeal over his child's birthday party

A local man has revealed the horrific ordeal he suffered at his child's birthday party.

Steve McDramagh wept uncontrollably as he described the harrowing experience which has left him broken both financially and emotionally.

Standing outside a local off-licence, the haggard father-of-three shook his head while muttering 'Baby Shark, do-do-do, Baby Shark'.

The 36-year-old and his wife decided to rent out a hall in the local community centre after their home destroyed during a birthday party last year.

'The wife wanted to have the party in our house but 'f**k that' I told her'.

'Last time, the wee b**tards smeared chocolate ice cream all over the living room walls until it looked like a Republican dirty protest', recalled Steve.

Despite this, Steve had an inkling the party would still be tortuous when his wife sent him up the M3 to fetch a balloon she'd won on a Facebook competition.

'We'd already spent about forty quid on balloons but she insisted that I drove half an hour to the Andersonstown Road for one'.

'A twenty-five mile round trip for a sack filled with a stranger's breath. Fucking mental', he moaned.

And things got even worse for Steve when his wife entrusted him with the sausage rolls.

'The party started at 4pm and there's me at ten past four in the house up to my ballix in puff pastry cos the b**tarding sausage rolls stuck to the oven tray', he recalled.

As a result, Steve arrived to his own child's party fifteen minutes late and endured the wrath of his pint-sized spouse, who spoke to him in front of their guests as if he was dog shite dangling from the sole of her size 3 shoe.

'The hall was unbearably warm. Like against the Geneva Convention warm', he remembered.

'And here I was trapped inside a dilapidated leisure centre surrounded by a tribe of hyperactive kids'.

'Some of them were repeatedly blowing on these miniature vuvuzelas and the rest were taking part in an unsupervised Battle Royal on a large inflatable structure in the corner of the room'.

Steve was then instructed by his beloved wife to assume the DJing responsibilities which involved blaring annoyingly repetitive songs at a deafening decibel level.

'Oh I spun all the classics' said Steve while shaking his head.

'What Does the Fox Say, Baby Shark and I'm a mother f**king Gummy Bear'.

Steve also recalled the bollocking his wife gave him for not having his phone ready at the moment when his daughter was blowing out the candles on her cake.

'I'd been so preoccupied with my birthday party related duties that I'd forgotten to eat'.

'So I lifted a flump from the sweetie stall to boost my sugar levels when suddenly I was being called all the b**tards under the sun for not having my camera ready'.

But Stevie says he wouldn't have it any other way.

'Before the kids, I led such a shallow existence'.

'I'd do things like see my friends and sleep for more than three consecutive hours'.

When asked if there was anything about his old life he was particularly glad to see the back of, he said:

'Getting my hole'.

Taxi driver goes on rampage after being asked: 'Ya busy the night, mate?'

A taxi driver is running amok through Belfast after revealing he 'couldn't take any more customer small talk', it has emerged.

Big Sandy McBickle, who does the evening shift for a local firm, went 'fuckin boo-ga-loo' after he was asked the same question asked by every customer who's entered his cab for the last 18 years.

At his wits end, McBickle abandoned his vehicle on the Upper Newtownards Road and embarked upon a violent rampage across East Belfast, during which he made sardonic observations on life.

We traced McBickle down to a petrol station which he was holding up at gunpoint, after he was told he would need to spend a minimum of £5 before he could use his bank card.

"Every b**tardin' night for the last 18 years I've had to endure the same three b**tardin' questions", explained Sandy.

"It starts off with 'Are ya busy the night mate?', swiftly followed by 'What time are ye on til?'".

"Then they'll start about what's on the radio and ask me 'Do ya like that there music, do ye?'".

"For the better part of two decades I have politely answered their questions but tonight I just snapped".

"So I says til him, 'No, I do not like the fucking Osmonds'"

"But I'd rather listen to Freddie Kruger slowly drag his claw down a blackboard or my Ma ridin' my Da - than engage you in a conversation – ya c**t ye".

After pistol whipping the shopkeeper and leaving the petrol station with under £5's worth of goods, McBickle hijacked a car and drove along the Ballysallagh Road only to find it was closed off again.

McBickle got out of his car and flung the 'Road Closed' sign into a nearby field like a discus before reaching a maintenance crew who were making repairs to the bridge.

"Here's a wacky idea lads", screamed Sandy.

"See instead of continually repairing this bridge and closing the roads off, why not just tear the b**tard thing down!?".

"There's about as much point in that bridge as there is to a porn storyline! Who even fucking uses it? Everyone is continually inconvenienced just because Lord Marblemouth walks his cows across it once every leap year? Wise the f**kin bap!'

McBickle then took out a rocket launcher and blew the useless stone structure to smithereens in order to prevent any more lorries from having their roof ripped open like a can of tuna or commuters being late for work.

"What d'ya fancy for dinner the night"

A local couple have begun their weekly ritual of repeatedly asking each other what they would like for from the take-away.

Sally-Lea Small and her husband, Dave, find themselves embroiled in the same eight hour long debate every Friday.

After the sort of back & forth that would leave even The Chuckle Brothers frustrated, extremely fussy Sally will utter the immortal line, 'Ach, just get me anything'.

"Get me anything, she said", said Dave.

"When we all know fine well, even the slightest mistake on my part will result in a Mariah Carey-esque meltdown", he sobbed.

Dave proceeded to give us some insight into their weekly barney.

"It'll start off jovial enough, you know, a wee text like 'what do you fancy love?' and then she'll say, 'Oh, I dunno, what do you fancy?'"

"Then, after a string of Whatsapp messages, texts, private mails and phone calls, she'll come off with something ridiculous like, 'I fancy something really nice tonight' - as if the rest of the week she's been force-feeding herself dog-shite sandwiches".

"Then I'll rhyme off a list of things I would like, ya know Chinese, Indian, Italian but each one is swiftly rebuffed without explanation".

"After she's rejected every take-away within a ten mile radius, she'll hit me with, 'Awk just get something. I'll eat anything'".

When asked how the situation is resolved, Dave told us:

"Once we've read all the forty-two menus in the drawer from cover to cover, we'll just order the same shite from the same place we do every week".

Woman who replaced toilet roll must want an OBE, claims husband

A local woman who replaced a toilet roll is acting as though it warrants an honour from the Queen, according to her husband.

Angel Soft (37) went 'fucking ape-shit' upon discovering that her husband, Scott (39), had used all the toilet paper again and 'never bothered his lazy hole' to replace it.

'All I heard was the yelling coming from upstairs', recalled Scott.

'So she put a new shit-roll on the wee metal arm thingy. Big deal. What's she after? A fuckin' Knighthood or something?' quizzed Scott, while sprawled along the sofa with a bowl of Doritos nestled between his hairy tits.

However, his long-suffering wife Angel unsurprisingly had a different interpretation of the events which unfolded.

'A cup of coffee ran right through me. Since I had our Justin, I just can't hold it in like I used to', she confessed

'I was boundin' uppa stairs two at a time and my gusset was ringin' like a Civil Service phone after 12 on a Friday'.

'Fortunately, I managed to get onto the toilet before I pished my good active wear'.

'But when I reached for the bog roll, all I could feel was the bare cardboard tube with a couple of wee strands hangin' off it'.

'Every day he locks himself in there for a good hour, shittin' like a horse with IBS and playin' Candy Crush on his phone'.

But it would never cross his mind to putta new bog roll on the holder when he's done'.

'He's a lazy fuck-dog. He doesn't lift a finger round here', she added.

However, Scott disagreed.

'Oh I lift a finger alright. My middle one as soon as her big back is turned', he sniggered.

'Your food's on its way, love', says lying b**tard.

A Belfast woman who works for a local take-away has been outed as a 'lying big bastard', according to reports.

Laura Lyons (42) is accused of deliberately misleading those customers trying to ascertain the whereabouts of their take-away meal.

Every night, Ms Lyons is bombarded with phone calls from impatient customers with terrible diets, demanding to know where their food is.

It doesn't matter if the food is out for delivery or if the driver is parked up miles away skinning a joint, Laura will always utter the immortal line, 'it's on its way, love'.

"I was a wee bit peckish last night so I ordered myself a donner kebab on chips, a 16" pizza and two litres of Coke", recalled local man Arty Harding

"She said it'd be about 45 minutes but when my grub wasn't here after 46 minutes I was straight on the dog & bone kickin' off".

'The auld doll on the phone said the traffic was bad or some ballix and the driver was on his way".

"What traffic? Sure it was 11 a'clack on a Sunday night".

"Anyways, 'bout half an hour later and still no sign of the fucker. So, I was straight back on the phone ta them".

"Nearly two hours he eventually arrives at my door and deliberately counts out my change like he's not wise til I lose the bap and tell him to keep it".

"When I opened the beg the bastards had forgat the garlic dip and the food was freezing".

"Fuck it, that's me eating sensible again. Back on the Herbalife l'mara", he added.

Man badly wounded after heading old football

A Dundonald man lost an eye whilst attempting to head an old leather football, it has emerged.

The 35-year-old father-of-two got involved in a 'kickabout' between local kids outside his home when the incident occurred.

Davy Blinker was raced to the Ulster Hospital where medics tried desperately to save his sight but unfortunately the damage was too severe.

The plumber was returning home from work when he spotted a group of local boys playing football outside his home.

Davy, who maintains he could've made it professionally if it wasn't for his 'bad knee', approached the boys and shouted: 'On the head'.

One young lad who plays for Glentoran U8s, whipped a ferocious cross towards Davy who rose like a salmon before planting a Duncan Ferguson-esque header past the hapless 5-year-old goalkeeper.

However, immediately after scoring the goal, Davy fell to his knees clutching his face and writhing around in agony.

Wee Harry Beckham who provided the cross recalled:

"Davy was pointing to where he wanted it and was thrusting his head back & forth like a chicken".

"With hindsight, given the terrible state of repair the ball was in, perhaps I did put a little too much venom on the cross".

"Because the jagged leather hexagons peeled the flesh off his forehead like someone was opening a mandarin orange".

Speaking from his hospital bed Mr Blinker told us:

"Aye I lost an eye but here, what a fuckin' goal. That's the way I used to score them for Fisher Body Seconds, so a did".

Mr Blinker was then joined in the ward by his next door neighbour Rab Sear.

Mr Sear was receiving treatment for 1st degree burns after his leg melted on a car exhaust when the same ball became stuck underneath it.

East Belfast Lazio fans target home of Roma fan

The escalating tensions between rival Serie A fans in East Belfast reached fever pitch last night, when offensive graffiti was sprayed on the home of a Roma supporter.

It's the latest in a series of clashes between supporters of A.S. Roma and S.S. Lazio which has left locals living in fear.

Roma fan, Big Franky Totti, woke this morning to find that his property had been daubed with the abusive slogan: 'Roma Scum'.

The 41-year-old owner of East Belfast-based car washing business 'The Karwashians' said:

"Last week I had my windies put in. Now this! Fuckin' Lazio bastards".

There's been an ongoing issue with Italian football related violence in the area ever since live Serie A games were screened here on Channel Four during the early 90s.

Chairman of the Grove Street Lazio Supporters Club, wee Sammy Signori, vehemently denies that any of their members were behind the attack.

"He probably did it himself", argued Sammy, whilst scrubbing the black paint of his hands.

Community representative Bobby Baggio has urged both sets of supporters to sit down together in order to bring an end to the violence.

"I would encourage fans of both teams to engage in constructive dialogue in order to find a resolution and avoid any sudden deaths or shootouts".

Meanwhile, in an attempt to diffuse the situation, the PSNI has appealed for offside.

89% of Northern Irish Millennials have never heard of a gravy ring

Most Millennials will have heard of Snapchat, emojis and dick-pics. But a 'Gravy Ring'? Not so much, according to a new study.

The Dundonald Institute of Pointless Research defines millennials as those who are between 20 and 35 years old.

Not only are they the largest generation so far, they're also the biggest pack of arseholes in the history of mankind

They think they know everything – but a study has revealed that they don't know what a 'gravy ring' is.

For those Millennials who are unfamiliar, a gravy ring is the correct Northern Irish term for a small fried cake of sweetened dough in a ring shape.

Yes, that's right. So if you've been calling it a doughnut or worse – donut, you're fucking wrong.

"The confusion between gravy rings and donuts occurred sometime during the 90s when The Troubles ended", said Prof Duncan D. Nutt of the Dundonald Institute.

"For years, everyone would go to a bakery and get served half a dozen gravy rings in a greasy white paper bag by a woman with bad teeth called Sylvia or Betty".

"But since the mid-ninties and the influx of American franchises like Duncan Donuts and Krispy Kreme, kids think they're called doughnuts"

"Bring back the shootin' and bombin', that's what I say", he added.

Nineteen-stone father-of-seven and gravy ring connoisseur, Patrick Baker, claims he stamped out such behaviour in his son early on.

"I told our Nathan, it's a gravy ring k'yid. A donut's got fuckin' jam in it".

"Then I clipped him round the lug. He never made that mistake again", beamed Patrick.

Provisional driving licences to allow bunny ears from 2019

The DVA has revealed that people applying for provisional driving licences in 2019 will be allowed to use Snapchat filters on their photos.

The agency announced the plans after they admitted normal photographic identification had been rendered obsolete.

"Most applicants will be 17-year-olds eager to write off their first car", said Ricky Peugeot of the DVA.

"We had a rake of forms sent in along with photographs of kids with giant eyes and foot-long rainbow coloured tongues".

"We were fighting a losing battle. If I had to stamp 'rejected' on one more application from a wee girl with a crown of flowers floating above her head, I was going off on the sick with stress", he added.

Meanwhile, the PSNI has confirmed that it will allow its officers to put Snapchat filters over mugshots in an attempt to boost flagging moral in the build up to riot season.

"There's nothing funnier than seeing a wee smick sporting a pair of bunny ears after lifting him for joyriding", chuckled Officer Goodfellow.

Local woman has just nipped out for a feg if the doctor calls her

A Dundonald woman asked a packed emergency room if they'd let the triage nurse know she was nipping out for a cigarette if her named happened to be called while she was outside.

Nicola O'Teen (52) visited her local accident & emergency department this morning complaining of a shortness of breath.

Mrs O'Teen, who has smoked from she was 8-years-old, was hoping they'd be able explain why she'd had such difficulty breathing of late.

The mother-of-three arrived in an ambulance shortly after 9am still clutching a twenty-deck of Superking Menthols.

"I tried ringin' a taxi but they said all their drivers were on jobs and they couldn't send one for fifteen minutes. So I rang an ambulance instead", explained Nicola.

"It had me here in less than five minutes plus I didn't have to pay a fare", she said with a cheeky wink and wry grin.

"I just kept my jammies on in case the big doc keeps me in", she added.

After finding a seat among the usual assortment of hypochondriacs, junkies and brawlers, Nicola glanced at the electronic noticeboard displaying the approximate waiting time:

"Four-fuckin-hours??? Here's me, 'Tell the doctor I'm outside having a smoke if they call my name out'. I'd look sweet sitting there for four hours without a feg", she barked.

While pointing in at the packed waiting room through the double doors, Nicola added:

"And there's fuck all wrong with half of them in there. I see them here all the time".

"How can I ruin dinner time tonight", ponders child

A local boy has spent the past hour pondering all the different ways he could make tonight's dining experience a living fucking hell for everyone.

Jacob Thompson usually ruins mealtimes at home with his unruly and unreasonable behaviour. This normally includes: refusing to eat; repeatedly falling off his chair and spilling juice.

However, the 3-year-old wannabe wrestler plans to shake things up this evening with some new disruptive and attention-seeking antics.

'Gotta freshen things up a little and keep my parents on their toes', said Jacob while sticking Lego up the dog's arse.

'I normally start off by demanding a different plate; a different cup; different cutlery. Then I'll ask for sauce. Then I'll tell them that they put too much sauce on my plate. So that's me onto my third different plate'.

'Sometimes, halfway through dinner I'll take myself off for a shite, then I'll call for assistance when I need my arse cleaned. I usually reserve that tactic when they're eating a meat and gravy based meal'.

'Last night the vein on the side of my Dad's head was very bulbous. I think if I can make him mad enough tonight that thing will burst', he added.

We caught up with Jacob's father, Frank (36), who was sat outside the family home in his car enjoying the last few moments of child-free peace.

'Sometimes I pretend I've to work late just so I don't have to eat with my child', confessed Frank.

'I can't remember the last time I ate a warm meal. It's been at least three years anyway'.

'I spend the majority of the meal watching him climb up on his chair and fall off. If I've to say 'get up' or 'get down' one more time I'm gonna change my name to James Brown', he added.

Couple to spend evening browsing Netflix without actually watching any thing

A Dundonald couple are looking forward to getting the kids to bed tonight then endlessly browsing through every movie on a popular streaming service until one of them either falls asleep or goes to bed in a huff.

Joe and Helen McMelter like to unwind at the end of an exhausting day of work and parenting by engaging in a three-hour-long debate about which movie they should watch.

However, in 9 out of 10 cases the indecisive pair will fail to reach agreement and end up watching fuck all.

'You pick something. I picked the last time', argued Helen.

'Sure no matter what I pick, you'll just say no anyway', countered Joe.

And so, after a toing and froing that'd give The Chuckle Brothers a sore head, Joe is left with the unenviable task of picking the movie.

'This is a bloody nightmare', said Helen. 'He's been up and down every genre from Dramas to Horror but still no agreement'.

'Look, it's 10.30pm already!! Now we can't watch anything longer than two hours or we'll be knackered in work tomorrow'.

'And it's a shite selection on Netflix anyway. Three quarters of the films have The Rock or Jason Statham in them and they couldn't act asleep'.

'Ach, just hurry up and pick something', barked Helen.

Three hours into the search and Joe's thumb was beginning to cramp and he complained of going cross-eyed.

'I'm not fussy, she says', moaned Joe. 'I'm not allowed to pick anything with zombies, aliens or John Travolta in it, cos apparently he gives her the shits'.

'So no doubt we'll end up watching some ballix like Dirty Dancing again. I can't believe women actually think it's a love story and there's Patrick Swayze's running about that summer camp collecting hymens like the Predator collected skulls'.

'Ach fuck this, watch whatever ya like, I'm away to bed', snapped Helen.

Man reveals ordeal after release from speed awareness course

A local man has described the horrific four-hour ordeal he suffered at a Speed Awareness Course after an emotional reunion with his family yesterday.

Martin Aston was trapped along with twenty-three others on an AA DriveTech course in Belfast for an unnecessarily long period of time.

The 36-year-old wept as the icy Northern Irish rain pelted his face for the first time in over four hours.

Scenes of jubilation erupted each time a course participant arrived to a hero's welcome outside Quay Gate House in the city.

Large video screens were set up in public places like Belfast's City Hall to let people watch and cheer as each person on the course was hauled to safety.

The participants were whisked away for medical check-ups and found to be in good health, except for one man who is feared to have lost both testicles to boredom.

Martin Aston broke down in tears as he told reporters about his harrowing experience:

'I never thought it would end. I'm just so happy to still be alive', sobbed Mr Aston.

'I'm not gonna lie. There were times I did think of giving up. There are only so many patronising videos of someone braking a Toyota Yaris a man can watch'.

The 36-year-old described how bibles, letters and pre-recorded messages from their families kept their spirits up during some dark and seemingly hopeless hours.

'I just kept thinking about the state my wife and kids would leave my house in if I wasn't there. That's what kept me going'.

Asked if he'd learnt any lessons from the experience, Aston replied: 'Definitely. I'm a shite driver so undoubtedly there'll be further speeding offences. But next time I'm taking the fucking points'.

Man's cold upgraded to 'bad cold'

A Dundonald man's cold has been upgraded to a 'bad cold' after a careful and thorough self-diagnosis, it has emerged.

Dave McDramagh (37) was 'sent home' from work yesterday morning such was the seriousness of his condition which had deteriorated further by the time his partner Helen arrived home from work.

She found her beleaguered boyfriend lying along the sofa under a quilt and 'texting around anyone he thought might give a fuck about his runny nose'.

By the evening Dave was convinced his condition had worsened further and feared things may have progressed to full-blown man-flu.

The 37-year-old then asked his girlfriend to fetch a pen and pad so that he might make a start on his will and testament.

'It's best I make the necessary preparations for the distribution of my property in the event of my untimely death', said Dave whilst wiping his nose with a Puffs Ultra Strong & Soft tissue.

'It's the least I could do to lighten the burden on Helen who has already had to witness the intolerable suffering I've endured', he uttered through a pained expression.

'She said that I've done nothing but moan since I Googled these symptoms'.

'But I've tried to explain to her that men don't moan. We emit involuntary groans which are directly proportionate to the excruciating pain we are in', he said.

'I told her I read online that the pains a woman experiences during child birth can become so severe that she almost knows what it's like to have 'Man-flu'.

'She was so overcome with sympathy, she accidentally spilled a scalding hot Lemsip all over my bollocks', winced Dave.

36-yr-old man still calls Ketchup 'red sauce'.

A Dundonald man broke down in tears this morning after admitting that he still calls tomato ketchup 'red sauce'.

Steve Hinds (36) made the confession shortly after making a complete fool of himself in a local Hipster burger joint, it has emerged.

The father-of-three was dining with his family in 'The Bearded Burger Emporium' yesterday afternoon when the incident occurred.

'The waitress had just put our food on the table and asked if we needed anything else', recalled Steve.

'I noticed there were no condiments on the table so I politely enquired about the possibility of getting some red sauce'.

'The waitress could barely keep a straight face. Even the kids were mortified', he sobbed.

'Red sauce is what I've always called it. It's easier and quicker to say than tomato ketchup', he explained.

Steve's children were so embarrassed by the whole episode that they've vowed never to eat in public with their father again.

'What a total ball bag that man is', raged three-year-old Sophie.

'You don't call mustard yellow sauce or mayo white sauce, do you? He needs to grow up. Any wonder I heard mum say she's thinking of leaving him', she added.

However, Steve remains undeterred.

'Mmm. Stew tonight. It's lovely with a bit of brown sauce in it', he said while painting a Warhammer figurine.

Terry's chocolate orange not one of your 5-a-day

Boffins at Dundonald Looniversity have made the startling discovery that a Terry's Chocolate Orange does not count as one of your 'five-a-day'.

This comes after another new study revealed that 9 out of 10 Northern Irish children are 'fat as fuck'.

Dr Oetker, head of research at Dundonald Looniversity, said, 'We carried out rigorous tests on our volunteer subjects, or 'lab fats' as we now call them'.

'Even though the Terry's version is divided into 20 segments, similar to real orange, and wrapped in orange-skin patterned foil – we can reveal it is NOT actually a real orange'.

The Terry's Chocolate Orange has been a mainstay in Northern Irish children's lunchboxes for thirty years and the news came as a surprise to many parents today.

'Am shacked. Totally shacked', confessed one mother in a Betty-Boop onesy outside a local primary school.

'You'd think they'd label these things a wee bit better. This is our children's health they're toying with here', said another mother while puffing on a Superking Menthol in a car packed full of kids.

Dr Oetker claims that other foods considered part of the Northern Irish diet wouldn't count towards the five-a-day target.

'Fruit Pastels, Strawberry Chewits and Pear Cider are also pretty bad for your health as it turns out', he said.

But not all parents are convinced of the new findings. Phil Inngs (37), told us he'd still be feeding his two boys 'proper grub' inspite of the recent warnings.

'Our Jacob was telling us this morning his teacher was worried about his diet. I hit him a good clip round the lug and told him to eat his Crème Eggs on toast', said Mr Inngs.

Mass confusion as 'troops out now' sparks calls for lad's night out

There was confusion in Belfast yesterday as new graffiti had hundreds of men demanding a night out with the boys.

'Troops Out Now' was found painted on at wall near a busy junction and the message soon spread to scores of men claiming to be oppressed and in dire need of a 'good session with the lads'.

'I dunno who wrote it but they're 100% spot on so they are', said married thirty-four-year-old Bazza Thompson.

'It's been donkeys since the troops were out on the rip. No one's allowed out anymore so they're not.', he added.

Bazza, buoyed on by the sentiment of the graffiti, created a secret Facebook group entitled 'Rockets on Tour' for his old pals and set about arranging an impromptu night out.

Much to Bazza's dismay, his calls for a piss-up were met with a lukewarm response, as many believed his proposal didn't afford them 'enough notice' and 'would be a hard-sell' to their other-halves.

'Bunch-a-fruits' said Bazza, when asked how his plans were going.

'All the excuses of the day I was hit with there, like 'it's my chile's 1st birthday the next day mate', so fuck, as if the wee shite's gonna remember if you were hangin' or not?'.

Furious, Bazza drove to the spot where the graffiti was and painted 'Troops NOT ALLOWED out now' beside it.

He was then set upon by an angry mob and is currently recovering in the Ulster Hospital.

Police alerted after possible Ugg boot sighting in Cultra

Police in North Down are appealing for anyone who may have seen a peasant woman wearing hideous sheepskin boots, it has emerged.

In a post on their Facebook page earlier today, they said: 'On October 6, 2017 at 11am Police received a report of what has been described as a large woman, most likely in receipt of government benefits, wearing horrendous tan fleecy boots, sighted in the Cultra area'.

The news sent shockwaves through the affluent residential area with many wondering how something so horrible could happen where they live.

Lady Ethel Marblemouth claims to have spotted the beast roaming the streets after some renovation work forced her to leave her home.

'We are having a waterfall feature installed in the fourth floor bathroom but the builders were making a frightful racket', explained Lady Marblemouth.

'So, I took Coco, our Chihuahua out for walk. Well, I got about 100 yards down the road and the next thing you know, this rotund peasant woman in sheepskin boots came bounding toward us'.

'I threw my jewells and cash at her and begged her not to stab us. Thankfully, she was distracted by something she was eating. It was something repulsive like sausage meat wrapped in puff pastry. The horror of it all'.

The PSNI then warned residents; 'If you do see an animal matching this description, contact the police immediately – DO NOT APPROACH!'.

Mervyns to be extinct by 2025 say experts

Northern Ireland's last remaining men named Mervyn will die off before 2025, scientists believe.

A study at Queens University suggests that males called Mervyn can now be classified as an endangered species.

Statistics show that Northern Irish parents in the 1940s named at least four of their sons Mervyn.

That figure dropped to two in the 60s and one by 1975.

A 'Mervyn' has been declared Northern Ireland's rarest breed of male, with only three individuals remaining – two elderly males and a 54-year-old transvestite.

All three are under armed guard at a conservation in Fermanagh.

'Unless there is a concerted effort by parents of new-borns, then I'm afraid that all Mervyns will become extinct within ten years', said tree-hugger Petal Jones.

'Look at these fine beasts', said Petal, whilst pointing at the three Mervyns in captivity.

'Look at their thick 70's UVF commander moustaches and Ulster Bus driver side-shades. Who wouldn't want to raise a Mervyn?'.

We asked some parents at the Ulster Hospital's maternity ward if they'd consider naming their babies Mervyn.

'F**k away off', said one heavily pregnant woman having a cigarette in her pyjamas outside the maternity department.

Portavogie brothers open peninsula's first gourmet herring bar

They're the identical twin brothers from Portavogie cooking up a storm with the news that they are to open the Peninsula's first café selling nothing but forage fish.

Billy Ray and Bubba McAuley (35), will open the doors to their bar, 'The Turtle's Head' next month.

The brothers are natives of a small County Down fishing port which has a population of 2,122 people, all of whom share the same three surnames.

The crest above the door of the town hall displays a hand with six fingers and a motto which reads, 'She's only your cousin from the front'.

'We did our market research and most people said they'd love a herring bar on the harbour', said Bubba McAuley, whilst sliding a bulging chippy-sausage-like finger up his left nostril.

'People can have their herring salted, smoked or pickled. All our herring sandwiches come with a choice of white bread, brown bread and inbred' drooled Billy Ray.

We were lucky enough to sample the boy's wares as they treated us to a sneak preview.

Our herrings were served on a roof slate caked in seagull shite and when we asked for a side of tobacco onions, Bubba presented us with an unpeeled raw onion and then proceeded to extinguish his cigarette on it.

Ards is overlooked by the impressive 125-foot high Scrabo Tower. 'It's second largest erection ever produced in County Down', exclaimed Bubba, 'the first being Billy Ray's when he saw Christine Bleakley in Poundland'.

Ards has been the setting for some notable movies, including Deliverance, a film about four men from Bangor 'West' who decide to spend the weekend canoeing in Portavogie Harbour, as well as The Hills Have Eyes franchise.

With their opening just a couple of weeks away, excitement is building with the worldwide interest in their venture.

'It's gone viral' said Billy Ray, 'just like the Herpes infection Bubba contracted last year'.

Thoughts and prayers go out to those affected by the KFC chicken shortage

As harrowing footage from across the UK floods in, leading politicians have offered their thoughts and prayers to the survivors of the KFC chicken shortage.

Millions of people woke up to the devastating news yesterday that fried chicken chain 'KFC' had somehow managed to run out of their primary ingredient.

It's a major embarrassment for the fast food giant whose famous Drive-Thru facility prides itself on its '100% guarantee of a ballsed up order'.

Theresa May led the tributes when she Tweeted: 'Our thoughts and prayers are with the victims and the families and friends of all those affected by this chicken shortage. We will re-stock'.

Shadow Home Secretary Diane Abbott added: 'My heart goes out to everyone associated with Kilmarnock Football Club today #jesuiskfc'.

900 outlets across the UK remain closed depriving millions of clammy out-of-breath people of their primary food source.

A recent High Street price comparison study revealed that a bucket of fried chicken parts and two litres of Sprite is cheaper than a punnet of strawberries.

'Deep-fried chicken is a staple diet for many piss-poor working-class yobos who cannot afford imported organic fruit and vegetables', explained Michael Gove, Secretary of State for Environment, Food and Rural Affairs.

One mother described how the store closures left her son in a coma. She said, 'Our Nathan's blood type is KFC Gravy Positive. The shutdown has left him comatose'.

'I tried pouring Bisto down his neck but it didn't work. The doctor said it's touch and go whether he'll pull through', she sobbed.

Riots erupted across major UK cities when it was announced it was unclear when the delivery problems would be rectified.

Last week, the fried chicken chain switched its delivery contract and blamed "operational issues" for the supply disruption.

Head of Internal Affairs, Wee 'mental' Mark Magee explained, 'It's all those'ns at DHL's fault apparently. But what the fuck would I know? I was working on the Drive-Thru last week'

In a case of mistaken identity, KFC counter staff have had their homes targeted by local 'Paedo Hunters' who thought the white-haired bearded man on their uniforms was in fact Rolf Harris.

Parents being force-fed inedible school pancakes

Parents across Northern Ireland are being forced to eat awful misshapen pancakes made by their children in school today, it has emerged.

Pancake Tuesday is an annual tradition observed in Northern Ireland which celebrates King Billy's victory over King James in a pancake eating contest in 1689.

Every year, teachers keen to avoid a proper day's work, bring out the mixing bowls and allow their pupils to make malformed vile pancakes instead.

Jack Flap (39) recalls last year's pancake day when his son Jack Jnr (6) arrived home from school proudly clutching a sandwich bag containing four sweaty deformed crepes.

'I thought I was gonna have to lick the dog's arse just to get the taste outta my mouth', explained Jack.

'They weren't fit for human consumption but what can you do, eh? Wee Jack was stood there all pleased with himself for making them'.

'He watched me like a hawk and wouldn't leave the room until I'd eaten all four of the bloody things'.

'I couldn't bring myself to swallow any of it. My cheeks were bulging; I looked like a hamster with gum abscesses'.

'As soon as he left the room I spat it out into the bin and gargled Domestos. I'm gonna write a letter to the school or knock his teacher's ballicks in. Probably the latter', he added.

Jack Jnr's teacher, Jonny Cake (41), readily admits that he's never sampled any of the children's crepes.

'Are ya f**king mad? Their heads are crawling in lice, their finger nails look as though they've been burrowing for truffles and they're stood in pairs sneezing into the baking bowls all morning'.

'I'd rather suck a handful of piss-dripping urinal cubes', he added.

PSNI smash Ballycastle 'Yellaman' cartel

Yellowman or 'Yellaman' with a street value of £22.50 has been seized by police in a property in Ballycastle, it has emerged.

A PSNI spokesperson said: 'A 55-year-old female and a 26-year-old male were arrested at a property on possession of a Class A Sweet with intent to supply'.

Yellowman is a highly addictive substance sold in non-standard blocks and chips.

It's produced when fuckin' mental amounts of golden syrup and sugar mixture are heated at high temperatures until the product reaches what is known as the 'the hard-crack'.

It first saw widespread use in primarily impoverished bucket and spade shit-holes such as Millisle during the 1980s.

Mass-production and wholesale distribution of the product is the responsibility of the notorious Ould Lammas Cartel based in Ballycastle.

The number of people becoming hooked on the chewy toffee-textured drug has skyrocketed in recent months, with some politicians calling it a 'pandemic'.

Just yesterday, a half-naked man was found in the toilet of a Ballycastle chippy by staff after having OD'd on 'yella racks'.

The amount of addicts requiring dental treatment is putting an unprecedented strain on local services. Local dentist Phil Inngs told us:

'I haven't had a day off in months. If I wanted to work my balls off I'd have done medicine mate'.

'They're coming in off their faces on 'Yellaman' with their teeth mangled. They make the guests on the Jeremy Kyle show look like fuckin' Colgate models'.

'To offset the cost, we had to hike our prices up for our one client who actually pays for his treatment'.

'He only came in for a clean-up this morning and had to apply for a Wonga loan to help cover the bill'.

A PSNI spokesperson added:

"We will continue to proactively tackle the issue of illegal tooth-breaking sweets.

"I would appeal to anyone who is aware of any individual involved in the supply of 'Yellaman', 'Blackpool Rack' or 'Highland Toffee' to contact their police on 101.

Investigation launched after man finds traces of meat in his kebab

An investigation is underway after a man found his 'post-sesh' meat-shavings were contaminated by real animal flesh.

Donald Babb, 23, made the grizzly discovery after running a series of tests on some leftover donner kebab meat.

The medical student's suspicions were aroused the next morning when he didn't feel any self-loathing or have an arsehole like a Roman Candle.

The shocking test results revealed that Donald's kebab contained traces of actual lamb meat, which may have contributed toward his unusual post-kebab experience.

'A typical take-away kebab consists of baboon arse-cheek (17%), chicken ovaries (23%), horse dick (30%) and greyhound (30%)', explained Don.

'The various animal parts are boiled then mixed with glue and sodium batteries, which gives you that debilitating gut-rot sensation the next day', he added.

Don immediately reported his findings to Trading Standards who promised to conduct a swift and thorough investigation into the matter.

'We received a report that a local kebab shop was serving customers actual lamb. We take these allegations very seriously'.

'An inebriated man should be able to stagger into his take-away and point at the slowly rotating chunk of compacted animal testicle – safe in the knowledge it doesn't contain actual meat', said a spokesperson for UK's Food Standards Agency.

Arslan Yılmaz, owner of the establishment in question, 'Arslan's Sweaty Meats', said, 'What do yousens put in your pasties? All the best organic ingredients I presume? Yiz Racist bastards?'

'A letter came in the post for you, will I open it?' asks local mother

A local woman sent a text message to her son this morning asking if he'd like her to open a letter which had arrived for him in the post.

Sally Pryer noticed the letter addressed to her son, Paul, which was clearly marked as confidential when sorting through her own mail.

Unbeknownst to Sally, Paul had forgotten to take his phone to work with him this morning.

The 61-year-old housewife claims she waited patiently on a reply for 'a good minute and a half' before deciding to open the envelope anyway.

Much to Sally's horror, the letter addressed to her beloved son was from a local genitourinary medicine clinic that revealed he'd tested positive for chlamydia.

When Paul (32) returned home from work this afternoon, he found his mother unconscious in the front hall still clutching the letter.

When he realised what had occurred, Paul suffered a severe panic-attack which lasted more than fifteen minutes.

'Usually it's just my bank statements and phone bills she reads. But how am I supposed to her look in the eye after this?', questioned Paul.

'It's an invasion of my privacy. I was so annoyed about this earlier I even contemplated moving out and paying all my own bills but then I came to my senses', he added.

Speaking while lying along the sofa with a cold flannel on her head, Sally said, 'I thought he'd got himself into debt or something. Little did I know his dick's been leaking like a butcher's bin bag'.

Men organize 'kickabout' after reminiscing about the good old days

A group of men were forced to have a 'kick-about' in their old neighbourhood after reminiscing about 'the good old days' on Facebook.

To the horror of the others, one friend took the empty gesture of a reunion literally and went ahead and organised a game of 5-a-side football on the grass bank where they used to play as children.

After a month and a half of organising, then reorganising because everyone's kids kept getting sick, the ageing gang finally met up on their old green to have a 'friendly' game of football.

'Wee Squazza', real name David Lemon (35) and once a flying wing-wizard, is now a fifteen stone father-of-three with cartilage damage in his left knee.

'We were having an aul rake on Facebook about the good aul days playin futball on the green. Someone suggested meeting up for a kick-about, I can't remember, it might have been me. Anyway, everyone was content in the knowledge that it would probably never materialise', said Squazza.

'That was until Stevie got involved. The next thing he was setting up Facebook groups and sending us spreadsheets. That's when we realised it was going to fuckin' happen', he added.

As kick-off approached, the men discussed the various aches and pains from which they were suffering before realising they had uneven numbers.

'We let Smicker and Dinger pick the teams cos they were the best players back in the day', explained Squazza

'I dunno if that's still the case though cos Smicker is nineteen stone and Dinger's type-2 diabetic now', he added.

'Just like years ago, wee Spud was the last player to be picked. Neither side wanted the tube in their team and there was a bit of row about it'.

'It continued until Spud broke down in tears and told us how much it used to hurt his feelings'.

Spud explained, 'They probably never thought much about it at the time but it's hard to put into a sentence how much of a crippling blow it is to your self-esteem, to watch a group of your peers almost come to blows over how little they want you to be in their team'.

About the game itself Squazza told us, 'The game started off in good spirits but things soured quickly'.

'There was an argument about whether a shot was 'in' or 'hit the post'. I said it was 'in' but in fairness it was hard to tell because the post was eight foot wide and made out of jumpers'.

'Then there was a huge row because I hit a shot which was flying into the top corner and Smicker stuck his hand out and stopped it. Then he tried to say it was 'fly-nets' - but no one called that at the start'.

'In a huff, I kicked the ball away and it rolled down the road onto the carriageway'.

'Smicker shouted 'hitsys getsys' but I refused to go get it. We squared up over it. But then we both realised we'd to go to work the next day and didn't want any marks on our faces'.

'Then a car ran over the ball. It turned egg-shaped and bounced funny. But by that stage everyone had 11 missed calls from their wife and had to leave anyway', he added.

Local gang confronts suspected Predator

An angry mob confronted a man in the Dundonald area whom they believe to be a Predator, it has emerged.

A video viewed thousands of times online shows the beast facing accusations from a vigilante group.

The man was accused of arranging to meet a human decoy, who they believe he intended to kill; skin and decapitate, before converting the carcass into a trophy.

The group recorded the sting on a mobile phone whilst they presented the towering brute with the mountain of evidence they had compiled against him.

Addressing the baying mob on his porch, the man exposed his arthropod-like mandibles before shouting, 'Fuck away off round yer own door'.

The crowd then drew various weapons including knuckle-dusters, baseball bats and a M134 six-barrelled machine gun, which they claimed were for the Predator's own safety.

The man then activated what eye-witnesses described, as some sort of camouflage cloaking device before scaling the wall of his three bedroom semi.

However, a spokesman for the PSNI last night confirmed that an arrest was made.

'A 49-year-old man was arrested on suspicion of attempting to remove a man's skull. But after a chat down the station, all the boys were satisfied this man was NOT a Predator'.

The spokesman also had a message for these so-called hunter groups.

'For fuck sake, knock it on the head. You're making us look bad'.

Local do-gooder taking selfies with homeless people again

A Dundonald man who uploaded a photo of himself handing a six inch 'Sub of the Day' to 'a poor old begger' is adamant that he wasn't fishing for likes, it has emerged.

Kyle Goodman, 23, was walking through the town centre when a homeless man made the terrible mistake of asking for 'spare odds'.

The beleaguered man's request gave Kyle a eureka moment and he sprang into action.

'If I'd gave him money he probably just would've spent it on something ghastly like booze or a blow job off a heroin addict', explained Kyle.

'So I went in and got him a 6-inch Sub and a hot drink instead. I sat down beside him for a chat and tried to establish – in a totally unpatronizing way – why he was lying in the street caked in his own shite'.

'While he was describing how the bank sold him a 125% mortgage he couldn't afford then seized his home, I decided to share his story without his consent on the internet', Kyle added.

'So I whipped out my iPhone X and took a selfie with him. The sun must've been in his eyes or something cos he was putting his hand across his face'.

The homeless man, Frank Hobo (42), although very grateful for the six inch Meatball Marinara, had an inkling he'd end up in a longwinded Facebook post.

'While I was telling Kyle about the perils of sub-prime lending, I could tell his mind was elsewhere. It was almost as if he was writing that Facebook post in his head instead of listening to me', said Frank.

'If I was a suspicious fella, I'd say Kyle was using me a pawn in some despicable scheme to make himself out to be a hero and maybe get his hole out of it. But hey, at least I don't have to wank someone off for grub today'.

Selfish bastard sets multiple alarms in the morning

An inconsiderate prick set multiple alarms from 6am this morning despite the fact he didn't get out of bed until nearly 8, it has emerged.

Joe Cockerel, 29, sets at least eight alarms at fifteen minute intervals every morning much to the annoyance of his partner Helen McMelter.

'He's a thoughtless selfish fucker', moaned Helen.

'He's absolutely no intention of getting his lazy hole outta bed at 6 o'clock in the morning, so I dunno why he insists in having the whole house up from that time?'.

'He just knocks it off and is snorin' again like an asthmatic walrus in a couple of seconds. But you know what I'm like, that's me wide awake', she added.

While Helen was sat on the sofa nursing a cup of coffee, barely able to keep her eyes open, Joe came bounding down the stairs full of life and whistling the Match of the Day theme tune.

'There's no way I could get up straight away', said Joe with a slice of toast in his mouth and jogging on the spot.

'I need to ease myself into the morning gradually. The brain's an engine, it needs to warm up'.

'I mean, look at the kip of thon on the sofa', he scoffed whilst pointing at Helen. 'She only sets one alarm in the mornings and look at the state of her? Eyes on her like a new-born rat'.

'The longer I live with that fucker, the more I realise I'll need an onion in my pocket at his funeral', concluded Helen.

Woman who said she didn't want anything from the shop actually did

A Dundonald woman who told her boyfriend that she didn't want anything from the shop went 'absolutely ballistic' when he returned home empty handed, it has emerged.

Helen McMelter, 29, threw a fit as soon as her long suffering partner, Dave, returned from the local shop with a bag full of treats for himself.

Before Dave left the house, he rhymed off a list of snacks that Helen usually loves but each of his suggestions were swiftly rebuffed by his stroppy girlfriend.

However, the moment Dave walked in through the door Helen demanded to know what was in the bag for her.

'What did you get me? She says', moaned Dave.

'A good fuckin' fifteen minutes I spent licking her hole before I left the house, practically begging her to get something. But no matter what I suggested, she barked, 'I said I don't want naffin', back at me.

'Then, as soon as I walk in with a bag fulla munchies she demands to know what's in there for her. She's my boiler pure busted so she does', he added.

'I know I said I didn't want naffin but he still shouda got me somethin', explained Helen.

'What was he thinking? That he was gonna sit there firing those fizzy sweets down his fat neck and I was gonna look down his throat?'

'He shoulda got me a slab of Dairy Milk for a wee cuppa tea later. Selfish bastard he is', added Helen.

But before Dave could put his arse to a seat, Helen sent him back to the shop.

'Get me a wee surprise, she says. No doubt I'll lift the wrong thing and that's me sleeping on the sofa', sobbed Dave.

Queens uni student recovering well after GAA top amputation

A Belfast student is said to be in a stable condition after undergoing an operation to have his Gaelic jersey removed.

The 19-year-old is recovering well in the Ulster Hospital after the complicated five hour procedure.

Sean McCulchie was admitted to hospital yesterday after his Antrim GAA shirt became fused to his flesh.

The garment attached itself to Mr McCulchie's body after he'd worn it every day since the beginning of the term.

Speaking from his hospital bed, Mr McCulchie told us, 'The surgeon told me there'd be some permanent scarring but he managed to remove around 95% of my Gaelic jersey'.

Lying in an adjacent bed was 37-year-old Celtic fan Jock Johnston who had recently underwent a similar procedure to have his Celtic FC shorts removed after wearing them for fourteen consecutive days during an all-inclusive holiday in Santa Ponza.

Mr Johnston, who was left with 78 stitches, thought he had avoided any fusing as he had taken some preventative measures at the end of the first week.

'After about 7 days, I swapped from the home shorts to the away shorts. I thought that'd stop them fusing to the skin. With hindsight, I maybe should've stuck the 3rd kit on as well'.

These operations follow on from similar procedures carried out on flute band members, who had worn their band uniforms for periods of up to five months.

Love Island viewer recovering well after brain removal

A young female Love Island viewer is expected to make a full recovery after having her entire brain removed, according to an update from doctors.

Leanne Carlisle had the surgery in a bid to appear on the next series of the show after TV execs were concerned about her ability to string sentences together.

'Me very confident me be on show now me have no frontal lobes', slurred Leanne whilst drooling heavily into a bedpan.

The 26-year-old from Belfast made an unsuccessful attempt to be a contestant on the current series of the show.

She recalls the rigorous testing that hopefuls were put through as they competed to perform on the reality programme.

'They make us do a four piece jigsaw of apple and put right shape in right hole', said Leanne while foaming at the mouth.

For anyone with dignity who hasn't watched the show, Love Island is

ITV2's latest revival of an exhausted reality format.

'It's boy meets girl, boy dumps girl, girl snogs ¬another boy, girl dumps other boy, boy gets back with girl, girl dumps boy, only to be dumped by boy, who gets back with other girl – and in the end they all get aggressive yeast infections', said a show producer.

Leanne's brother Ryan is also on the waiting list for an NHS brain removal as he too hopes to appear on the show.

Ryan, who refers to himself as Ryan 'the brand' Carlisle, has over 120 followers on Instagram and spends his days in front of the mirror practicing the expressions, 'mugged off' and 'pied'.

'Most of the women in the show have a higher sperm count than the fellas. I can't wait to get in there and increase their dosages', beamed Ryan while buttoning up his white jeans.

7 HALLAWEEN

Queue starts outside Elliotts

Hundreds of people have started gathering outside the doors of Elliott's costume shop in Belfast's Ann Street in order 'to beat the mad queues', it has emerged.

Every October, a snaking queue approximately fourteen kilometres in length, forms outside the long-standing city centre business.

Even though the shop is open all year round and Halloween has been celebrated every October 31st since 1745, people flock to the shop in their droves in the couple of weeks leading up to the holiday.

Last year revellers found themselves in the queue for periods of up to six days and were kept alive by humanitarian aid.

Among the customers at Elliotts last year was Civil Servant Sammy Idle.

Sammy told us, 'We were having a house party this year. The Mrs was on my case big-style about some nauseating matching costume so I said I'd nip round to Elliotts on my lunch break for a wee nosy'.

'I thought there might be a wee queue but being a Civil Servant I can take up to a 5 hour lunch so I thought I'd be fine'.

'To my horror I joined the back of the queue in somewhere in Ballymena'.

'I didn't get out of the shop until 4th November and missed Halloween. She was absolutely fuming so she was'.

When asked what his wife was for Halloween, Sammy replied: 'Same as last year. A bastard'.

Thirty-something 'Death Metal' t-shirt wearing couple Stu and Allison queued up today so they'd have their Suicide Squad costumes in time for the holiday.

Stu said, 'I suggested we go as something Gothic this year but Allison insisted she was dressing up as Harley Quinn'.

'But when she stuck it on she looked more like Robbie Coltrane than Margot Robbie'.

A Dundonald guide to 'Hallaween' in the 80s

Hello, and welcome to my guide to Hallaween in 1980s Dundanal.

Back then, a chile in Dundanal would get more excited about Hallaween than they did about Chrismus. It was the one day a year they could dress up as ler favrit superhero and be that person for the whole day.

But nine tymes outta ten, despite bein promised they were getting a He-man costume, ler granny wud take lem down la Newtownards Road on the No8 bus and get lem a 50p false-face outta fuckin' Glovers or Cheepers.

Those false faces wor attached to yer head by a ridiculously tight elastic string which wud often cut the circulation off after a wile. The hard plastic casing had two piss-holes ya cud see fru and sometimes if the plastic gotta wee nick in it, you'd lacerate the fuckin' bake clean aff yourself.

If you'd enough of slicing yer bake with the aul false-face, ya cud always ram in the 'one size fits all' vampire teeth yer granny bought ya. Unless yu'd a fuckin' gob on ye the size'a Mick Jagger's, yer mouth was ripped open like thon Joker fella in the Dark Knight.

Once you'd rammed the plastic teeth in, some relative wud come over with the aul 'Vampire Blood'. This here dark red liquid wud permanently stain anything it would come into contact with and came in a wee bottle which had no health and safety warnings on it. Yet here was yer aul aunt Ethel squirtin the fuckin shit in yer mouth and eyes.

While she was down in Glovers and Cheepers, yer granny wudda spent la rest of her bru money on 6ft cardboard Draculas and skeletons. Then every bawsterd wud stick lem to the walls and ceilings using brass tacks, totally wreckin the wallpaper and plaster work.

Yu'd all play games like 'duckin for apples', which was the least hygienic game in modern history. A house fulla dentally challenged people fishin apples outta a basin fulla water usin only ler putrid aul mouths. After the whole post code had ler bakes in it, the water to saliva ratio stood at 2:8.

Another unsafe thing to give young childer was an apple tart fulla some of the biggest bastardin' coins ever minted. The odd time someone would choke on a 50p and they were told, 'fuck up and stop complaining you ungrateful wee shite'.

Apples hangin from the ceiling which you had to eat with your hands behind your back wuz another cracker. I don't know what hurt more, the misdirected head-butts or occasionally that the apple would swing away and come back to smack you in the teeth like a big cider tastin' wreckin ball.

Then yu'd take a wee race down to Tommy's van. The type'a neighbourhood convenience that existed before the likes of Centra. It sold sweets, WWF stickers, fake fegs that had been dipped in ammonia and most importantly, Bengal matches. Am nat really sure lat sellin a bax'a matches til a chile was a great idea. In fairness, he did ask me if I was 16, even though I was clearly only 8.

Then yer ma wud hand ye a pack'a 'Sparklers'. A metallic rod covered in an explosive that could reach 2,000 degrees Celsius. And there's you prabably wrapped in a bin-beg - but 'fuck it' she'd say, 'there's a full pack - and an aul lighter. You and yer brother have a ball luv'.

Then the real fireworks would come out. Yer granda wud get a bax off some dodgy cunt in work coz the peelers banned lem at the time. Then the 'hard mawn' of the street wud stick some rackets inside a milk battle and light lem - while the rest of the street wud duck behind ler fences as if it was the fuckin' launch of Apollo 13 or sumfin.

Then you'd all go out with your carved turnips (pumpkins were for 'snobby bawstards') you'd bought in Wellworths and go 'knockin la doors'. 'Knockin la doors' is the same as 'Trick or Treating' - but if you saidsomethin' gay like that in Ballybeen circa 1987 yu'd have gat yer ballix knocked in so ya wud. It was also something you could do unsupervised in those days, without the fear of being dragged you away by someone yu'd now see doorstepped in a Predator Hunters sting video.

At the end of la night the whole house stank. Yer granda would be sittin in la corner carving a turnip and your granny wud say ta ye, 'I'm sick of that smelly aul vegetable - and the turnip'.

'Don't f**king touch it, you'll ruin it', kids told.

Children across Northern Ireland are looking forward to another year of watching their parents carve elaborate designs into pumpkins, it has emerged.

Since the start of the decade, the age-old Halloween tradition of pumpkin carving has taken on a life of its own by becoming some sort of online cock-measuring contest.

Nowadays, competitive arse-holes enjoy whittling intricate designs into foul-smelling orange-yellow fruits using templates they downloaded from the internet.

However, despite claims that 'it's all about the kids', children are absolutely forbidden to participate in the carving in case they ruin it.

'Oh goody. Another year watching Dave attempt a Xenomorph from the Aliens franchise', grumbled 8-yr-old Jack O' Landon.

'He's gone all out this year and ordered proper tools off the internet'.

'I just heard him call some of the other Dads very rude words after he saw their pumpkins on Facebook'.

'Last year I sat and watched him for four hours straight before I called it a night at 1am'.

'He asked me where I was going and when I told him I was going to bed cos I was tired he called me an ungrateful bastard and threw a fist full of pumpkin seeds at me'.

'Bonfires, pumpkins, sofas full of presents on Christmas morning - it's just a never ending cock-measuring contest these days', ranted Jack.

Meanwhile, Jack's grandfather Cecil scoffed when his son, Dave, sent a picture message of the finished article at 2am.

'F**king big girl's blouse wants to stop fannying about with those pumpkins and start gutting out turnips using a teaspoon'.

'That's how I got this third knuckle on my thumbs', he added.

Lazy bastard's pumpkin starting to rot

A lazy bastard's pumpkin is beginning to wither on his doorstep almost a week after Halloween, it has emerged.

Local man Bill Idle (38) placed a pumpkin he carved for his children at his front door last Wednesday evening.

However, almost a full week has elapsed since then and the rounded orange-yellow fruit has started to rot.

'I thought I'd leave the thing on display until after the weekend', explained Bill.

'Cost me about four hours of my time and the tip of my baby finger to carve the bastard'.

'There was no way I was going to all that effort then dumping it the next day'.

'I might lift it tonight after work if it's dry'.

'Or maybe the birds will it eat? Who knows? It's not a big deal', he added.

However, the weekend came and went yet the pumpkin is STILL on show outside Bill's house.

'It smells funny', winced Bill's 7-year-old daughter, Amy.

'It looks creepier now than it did last week. I wish that lazy bastard would put it in the brown bin before it gives me nightmares', she added.

'Please, kill me', whispered the pumpkin.

NI Parent's Outrage as Child's Terrorist Costume Has No Balaclava or Sovereign Rings

A Halloween costume for children has been withdrawn from a shop in Northern Ireland because 'it looks f**k all like one of our ones', it has emerged.

The £15 outfit features a camouflage jacket, long, black beard and Muslim headpiece.

Newspaper, The Coleraine Times, reports that the costume has now been withdrawn from a pop-up Halloween store in the town's Diamond Centre.

One angry dad said: "There's no way our Callum is dressing up like yer big man Sammy Bin Laden. If he's going to dress like a terrorist then he'll be wearing a balaclava and a bomber jacket out of Millets'.

'This is just another example of the erosion of the Northern Irish culture. Bloody foreigners. Comin' over here and taking over our terrorism'.

Another shopper, who complained that they found the outfit offensive, added: "Where was the green beret and the aviator sunglasses? Ok, there was some camouflage there but it was a bloody waistcoat. I could hardly wear that'.

Allister Lovely of the Alliance Party said, 'So it seems that just dressing up like a Muslim and having a beard means you look like a terrorist which sends out the message that all terrorists are Muslim. There are plenty of the scoundrels wearing Henry Lloyd jumpers and Henley t-shirts too'.

Big Tina thought the fact it's aimed at children makes it even worse. She said, 'Disgusting. Our Stacy will be going as something more appropriate like a slutty devil'.

Killer Clown Movement Thrown into Chaos as Leader Loses Virginity

The entire Killer Clown movement was thrown into turmoil last night as the leader of the cult finally lost his virginity at the age of 42, it has emerged.

Walter Coco's mother, Agnes, arranged for a prostitute to visit the home she shares with her son after she discovered a rainbow coloured wig and giant shoes under the single bed he sleeps in.

Long-suffering Agnes has endured years of humiliation at the hands of her son who spends his afternoons in the Games Workshop with pre-pubescent boys rolling dice around a large table.

While her son's peers left school and raised families of their own, Walter's greatest achievement was becoming a Level Three Night Elf of Azeroth in the online role-playing game World of Warcraft.

Widowed Agnes spent the better part of her fifties and sixties picking Walter's rock-hard sports socks off his bedroom floor and had resigned herself to the fact he would die a virgin.

However, the discovery of her son's clown costume made Agnes take drastic action and she made contact with a Chinese fellow who ran a brothel just off Castle Street in Belfast.

Agnes told us, 'I put up with washing socks like plaster of Paris for twenty odd years. But knowing your own son, a grown man, was roaming the streets at night dressed like a fuckin' eejit and trying to scare kids, that was the final straw'.

'I went uppa West and spoke to Mr Cheung. He sent a girl round to our house and about ten minutes later our Walter was lying star-fished on top of his Dr Who quilt like a Cheshire cat. Five minutes after that I heard him putting the clown costume in the black bin'.

In other news, the PSNI were alerted when a large posse of clowns were seen entering Stormont this morning.

8 CELEBRITY GASSIP

Brendan Dassey to face Ken Kratz at Wrestlemania 35

WWE supremo Vince McMahon has announced that convict Brendan Dassey will face former special prosecutor Ken Kratz at Wrestlemania 35.

The event will be available to stream via Netflix with the loser of the bout spending the remainder of their life in Columbia Correctional Institution, Wisconsin - without the chance of parole.

'Forget McGregor/Mayweather, this is the contest the world's been waiting for', beamed Vince.

'It's a 'Hell in a Cell' match with a twist - the loser will spend the rest of their life in jailllll', growled McMahon as the veins bulged in his neck.

The match represents Dassey's last realistic hope of freedom after the state of Wisconsin scuppered all his court appeals.

Dassey was just 16-years-old when he confessed to the murder of Teresa Halbach, his involvement in the JFK assassination and his role in the RHI Scandal while being interrogated by the police.

When asked if he was looking forward to facing Ken Kratz at Wrestlemania, Dassey replied 'Um, yeah'.

McMahon also revealed that Donald Trump has been appointed Special Guest Referee for the bout, scheduled to take place on April 7 next year.

While receiving his award for 'Biggest Bastard Alive' at a Comic Con, Ken Kratz told reporters:

'He can bring Steven Avery, Chuck & Earl, Ma Every - even his fucking cat to ring as well. But there is no way that kid will ever again see the light of day'.

Kratz then whipped off his shirt and tie before treating the assembled media to an impromptu pose down.

Shaggy strenuously denies cheating with next door neighbor

Jamaican popstar Shaggy has strenuously denied claims he made sexual advances toward the girl next door, it has emerged.

Despite a mountain of incriminating evidence, including being rumbled mid-act by his girlfriend, the 50-year-old released a statement denying that he was 'caught red-handed' while riding the life clean out of his neighbour.

In a brief statement posted on his personal Twitter account this morning, Shaggy AKA 'Mista Luva Luva', said, 'It wasn't me'.

The allegations come after years of rumours which have dogged the self-proclaimed 'Boombastic lover'.

Sources close to the star believe that in light of the damning evidence he should confess and accept the consequences of his actions.

One friend told us, 'He was bragging to everyone about how he was bucking his next door neighbour all over her house'.

'The kitchen counter, the sofa, the shower – you name it, big Shaggy bucked her in it'.

'What makes matters worse is that his missus scooped him while he was balls-deep in the neighbour. And he still has the brassneck to deny it. I'm scundered for him'.

161

The reggae singer's long-suffering partner Julie Mee sobbed, 'I even caught the bastard on camera and he still won't come clean'.

Bono visits Ballybeen survivors of Storm Ali

Rock saint Bono chartered a private jet to George Best Airport so that he could see first-hand the devastation caused to Ballybeen by Storm Ali.

Winds of up to 5mph swirled through the Estate this afternoon, resulting in the destruction of countless garden gnomes, three patio chairs and an old tree.

Harrowing images of residents clinging onto their trampolines were broadcast around the globe leading to an outpouring of sympathy as #prayforballybeen began trending on Twitter.

After witnessing the footage, Bono decided to intervene in the humanitarian crisis they're describing as the worst to hit Ballybeen since the Mace ran out of fegs last year.

'I'll be staging a charity gig in the Enler Complex with all the proceeds going towards the victims of Storm Ali', announced Bono.

'And this kind-hearted gentleman has offered to help collect donations for all of those in need', said Bono whilst pointing at a shaven-headed man shaking a bucket with one hand and restraining a rabid muscular dog with the other.

With many local businesses closing early due to safety concerns, many men sought refuge in the nearby Bowlers club.

All schools in Dundonald were closed – except for a card school, which experienced unusually high attendance figures.

Dundonald Independence Committee member Sammy Mellon was less than enthused to see Bono in the Estate.

'A hurricane is one thing but the thought of that insincere bastard singing into the camera with that constipated expression on his face is another'.

'Don't you think these kids have suffered enough?', he questioned.

God: I didn't burn down Primark

God has strenuously denied allegations that he burnt down Belfast's Primark store because of the company's LGBT links, it has emerged.

When the landmark Bank Buildings in Belfast city centre caught fire yesterday afternoon, some people alleged that our Heavenly Father was directly responsible.

Those circulating the rumours suggested the Almighty One wreaked his fiery revenge on the Irish retailer for placing some rainbow-coloured articles of clothing on display.

But the Holy Spirit finally broke his silence this morning to describe the allegations as: 'Total wank'.

Talking to Belfast Live, God said: 'Listen, I would never burn down Primark'.

'I'll admit, I considered it for split second last week when they put their Christmas jumpers on display but I didn't do it'.

'Do you know many prayers per week I get from men being trailed around that shop, asking me to set fire to it?'.

'But no matter how much they beg, I say, suck it up lads. No doubt she'll be stuck in the house tonight watching the football. Fair is fair'.

The Father and creator of the universe admits he was a tad vengeful in the past but those days are well and truly behind him.

'The flood was a bit of a watershed moment for me', he mused.

'After that I said to myself, no more genocides. I've definitely mellowed since then'.

When asked if the people of Northern Ireland should be sending Primark employees thoughts and prayers in the wake of the blaze, God replied: 'No, send them money'.

James Nesbitt just watching Frampton fight in the house

Coleraine's best living actor, James Nesbitt, has vowed to watch Carl Frampton's upcoming fight from the safety of his own home after some drunken antics at his compatriot's previous bouts.

The 53-year-old reportedly told friends, 'F**k it. I'm just gonna watch it in the house so I am'.

Thespian Nesbitt is famed for his portrayal of on-screen characters who aren't particularly attractive but seem to do a lot of riding.

But most critics agree the most memorable performance of his career came during a ringside interview at The Jackal's victorious fight against Scott Quigg in March 2016.

The Cold Feet star was necking pints of Black Bush when the SkySports cameras noticed he was off his tits and decided to stick him on live tv 'for the craic'.

Nesbitt proceeded to ramble on about the Northern Ireland top his aunt bought him for Christmas before licking Tony McCoy's face and shouting 'fucka peelers' down the microphone.

Everyone has ripped the back out of the Murphy's Law star ever since and so he's made the very wise decision to remain at home this Saturday night.

'If I go to the fight I'll only end up making a c**t outta myself', admitted Nesbitt.

'Then the next day the press will be sniffing round me like a German Shepherd near Michaella McCollum's suitcase'.

'I'm just gonna book the fight on Sky, unless you have any decent links?', he enquired.

'Obviously it's not as exciting as being ringside but at least I won't end up seeing my drunken bake on a thousand memes this way'.

When asked if he'd be getting a carry-out James replied, 'Na, that's me aff it'.

Pat Jennings asks barber for 'same again'

Northern Irish goalkeeping legend Pat Jennings has asked his long-suffering barber for the same haircut for the 650th time in a row, it has emerged.

The former Spurs and Arsenal 'keeper has been sporting the same hairstyle for an impressive fifty years, despite the protestations of his life-long barber and friend, Dessy Shears.

Earlier today, the 7ft Newry man visited Shears' and after a brief deliberation he mumbled, 'I'll just have the same as last time'.

'I've begged him for years to try something different', said Dessy. 'That style was ok about 1978 but now he looks like Alan Partridge's great-granda'.

When asked if Jennings had EVER considered a change of style Dessy recalled, 'There was this one time back in 1993 that Pat said he wanted me to cut it into curtains'.

'But by the time I'd put the apron on him he'd changed his mind'.

Jennings, who has an impressive wingspan of 3.6m, won 119 caps for Northern Ireland but according to Shears, Pat was never tempted to try one on, 'in case it wrecked his hair'.

Only last year, Jenning's shaggy hair-do was inducted into the National Football Museum after being deemed 'culturaly, historically and aesthetically signficant'.

Other inductees included a Maradona urine sample, Sir Alex Ferguson's 67 minute watch and Luis Suarez's ivory tusks.

Angelina offered flat in the West Winds

Angelina Jolie has been offered a flat in the West Winds Estate as her divorce from husband Brad Pitt rumbles on.

Jolie and her twenty-four children are currently staying at the Strangford

Arms Hotel whilst her application for a new dwelling is being processed by the council.

The actress and humanitarian also dropped a huge hint that she's packing work in by changing her job title on Facebook to 'Full time mummy'.

Meanwhile, her estranged husband Brad, 54, has moved back in with his parents and is rumoured to be planning a lad's holiday to Malia with George Clooney, Ed Norton and Guy Ritchie.

Locals are said to be furious that the millionaire actress is being given a flat and their anger intensified when they discovered that the Maleficent star had also applied for a crisis loan for a holiday.

One resident told us, 'Who does she think she is? Swanning in here and getting a flat straight away? What is it? Twenty-four kids by twenty-one different fellas? Absolute trollop'.

However, Strangford MLA Mike Nesbitt is delighted that Jolie was becoming a Newtownardian but admits he's still sad about her split from hunky husband Brad.

The former UUP leader took to Twitter this morning and said:

'Channel 5 was showing Mr & Mrs Smith last night and I'm not ashamed to say I cracked open a bottle of Pinot Grigio and had a good gurn watching it'.

'Like everyone else across the country, I just want to know why these two beautiful specimens of humanity have parted ways?'

When asked for her opinion on Jolie's relocation Jennifer Anniston said 'I can't even!'.

Proclaimers apply for a mobility car

Scottish duo The Proclaimers were seen in a car showroom picking out a mobility car, it has emerged.

It follows reports the ageing pair are no longer able to make their arduous five hundred mile trek on foot.

For over thirty years the brothers have bragged about the thousands of miles they've clocked up in pursuit of fanny.

But it would appear the gruelling sex-fuelled hikes have finally taken their toll on the singers as they were spotted leaving a Ford car dealership late yesterday afternoon.

Car salesman Dick Crook told us, 'I can confirm that two fairly similar looking Scottish lads were in here asking about mobility cars'.

'They were looking for a used car with low mileage and a decent MPG', he added.

Rumours about the brothers applying for Disability Living Allowance began circulating online late last year.

Identical twins Craig & Charlie Reid confirmed as much in a drunken expletive-laden tirade during a gig last month.

The Leith men bragged to stunned fans about how they were 'on the tap whack DLA'.

A source at the HMRC believes the 'King of the Road' singers may have exaggerated the severity of their conditions.

'The two bastards breezed through that medical. They knew every answer. Bad backs my bollocks', said our source.

'They're pro-claimers now alright', they added.

Prince Harry books table in Benedicts for stag do

Prince Harry is set to visit notorious Belfast nightspot 'Benedicts' as a part of his 'Stag Do', it has emerged.

Harry, fifth in line to the throne, instructed his Best Man, brother William, to ring Benedicts this morning and 'book a table for twelve'.

Benedicts Hotel, situated in Shaftsbury Square, is renowned for its great food, affordable rooms and hand-to-hand combat at last orders.

After making an official announcement this morning regards his engagement to 'Suits' actress Meghan Markle, Harry and William began making preparations for the stag do.

'William was on the ball right away', explained Harry.

'As soon as he heard about the proposal he was straight round to my gaff with a case of Carlsberg'.

'We got the laptop out and starting pricing flights. This delightful little Irish airline called Ryanair said they'd fly us to Belfast for thirty pounds, which was jolly good'.

'Wills set up a Whatsapp group and added all the usual cut-throats like Arthur Landon, Ricky Branson's son, Sam and Thomas van Straubenzee. The banter will be off the Richter scale', concluded the ginger Prince.

Brother William was equally enthused at the prospect of visiting one of Belfast's premier night spots. He said, 'I'm looking forward to engaging in a spot of fisty-cuffs with some of the Sunday night regulars from Sandy Row. It'll be terribly exciting'.

'We're getting T-Shirts made for the airport with our nicknames on the back and I've booked Harry a Northern Irish stripper called Pamela Ballantine', he revealed.

Meanwhile, Meghan Markle is also reportedly planning a Belfast 'Hen Do'. The 36-year-old actress told Vanity Fair, 'Me and the girls are thinking of hitting Alibi, all dressed in pink with fairy wings and holding a four foot inflatable cock'.

Bear Grylls survives three day trek along Connswater River

Bear Grylls, overgrown Cub Scout and habitual drinker of his own piss, is known for his death defying survival exploits across some of the world's most treacherous terrains.

His latest challenge saw him attempting to cross the Connswater river in a dingy with several members of the paramilitary organisation the

Dundonald Liberation Army.

The DLA council requested Grylls' help with survival skills after two of their soldiers got lost inside IKEA for three days.

'We were three broken, cold and very scared men, huddled together, a few feet offshore, in the middle of the Connswater river, in a small rigid inflatable boat', Grylls remembers of the experience,

Grylls steered his team past Lidls in 4ft deep of murky water as they navigated their way around shopping trolleys and shitty nappies. The men had almost ran out of water and food rations when suddenly they struck gold.

DLA man Winky Williams recalls, 'I was absolutely chokin so I was. Then yer man Bare Arse or whatever ya call him found what he thought was half a tin of Special Brew sittin on la wall. I tried to warn him it that it was probably fulla pish but that only seemed to get him even more excited'.

Grylls then poured the rest of the Special Brew into a makeshift canteen he'd fashioned out of a used condom.

Asked whether he drank any himself, Winky Williams replied, 'Fack away aff! I ended up drinking Connsy river water and spent three weeks in the Ulster with everything from Cholera to fuckin Bieber Fever'

The men were at the point of starvation when Grylls managed to source some food. He recalls, 'I've ate dung beetles, I've even eaten a camel's knob but nothing quite prepared me for the food that was served to me in the Connswater branch of KFC. I had to eat my own shite just to get the taste out of my mouth'.

As soon as Bear's back was turned the DLA men jumped out of the dingy and headed to the nearest bar. Winky Williams said, 'Yer man Bare Arse said he was going to find some food and told us to piss ourselves to keep warm if we had to. We pissed ourselves alright, pissed ourselves the whole way to the Albert'.

Kim & Kanye ask people respect their right to extra publicity following split

Celebrity duo Kanye West and Kim Kardashian have asked the public to respect their right to extra publicity following the breakdown of their marriage.

The couple have decided to spend some time apart after almost three years of never seeing each other due to their hectic schedules.

'Kanye has deleted his Twitter account and has decided to live on a mountain in Wyoming. Everyone on earth, including Kim, is delighted', reported TMZ.

Reports suggested the rapper, 38, had taken himself off to a remote mountain top in order to plagiarise another Curtis Mayfield album.

However, sources close to Kanye claim the singer is 'getting his head showered' as he struggles to deal with parenthood and his 'mental' in-laws, including Kim's big brother Khloe.

'Kanye doesn't think he should have to change Saint's diapers coz Kanye doesn't take shit from anyone', the source revealed.

Self-proclaimed genius West, also struggled to cope with the antics of his wife's family. Particularly his father-in-law Caitlyn Jenner, whom the rest of the family emasculated to the point he had his testicles removed.

'Kanye saw how Bruce was forced to sleep in a garage in his own mansion by Kris. Once Kim started complaining about Kanye's snoring, he knew it was only a matter of time before he appeared on the cover of Vanity Fair in a frock', added the source.

The 'Gold Digger' singer semi-retired from the music scene in 2010 so that he could concentrate on being a complete bastard but the break-up could spawn several more dreadful albums.

Meanwhile, not to be usurped in the attention stakes, Kim took a shite on her laptop and uploaded a photo of it to Instagram.

Unfortunately, the poo clogged some of the ports and she couldn't connect to wifi. 'Looks like I broke the internet again' giggled Kim.

Famous doggers demand privacy

A married celebrity who has been engaging in threesomes on the deck of his yacht in broad daylight, has asked us all to respect his privacy, it has emerged.

Elton John and his husband who can't be named for legal reasons, have wasted a lot of money trying to keep the latter's affairs quiet despite the fact that Twitter renders any super injunction more pointless than a breast with no nipple.

Sir Elton, 69, managed to secure his favourite type of order - a 'gagging' one - which prevented the upstanding citizens at The Sun Newspaper from publishing graphic details of the sexual romps in their self-proclaimed family newspaper.

Despite this, bloggers have been able to leak details of the affairs online causing much embarrassment to Elton who is said to be furious with his cheating spouse. Elton told us, 'David has been having a sex with a tiny dancer. He's yet to apologise. Sorry seems to be the hardest word'.

He went on, 'I've been so down lately I've been taking these wee blue tablets called Diazepam. I guess that's why they call them the blues. David walked out a week ago. But can't wait til the bitch is back so I can slap the bake off him'.

Elton is understood to be being comforted by Chelsea star John Terry who moved in with the Rocket Man singer immediately after Furnish moved out. Our source told us, 'JT just happened to be in the neighbourhood when he heard the awful news. John's been a real shoulder to cry on for Elton'.

They added, 'John took Elton out for a fancy meal to celebrate signing a new contract at Chelsea'.

When asked about his twelve month deal Terry said, 'I can't wait to work with the next three Chelsea managers'.

9 SPORT

Local man 'knows what's going through Frampton's mind right now' after Boxercise class

As Saturday's boxing bout between Carl Frampton and Luke Jackson fast approaches, a Belfast man claims to know 'exactly what Carl Frampton is going through'

Wee Davy Brawler, from Vionville Rise beside Tullycarnet, knows all too well about the sacrifices and dedication the sport requires after attending a couple of Boxercise classes at his local gym.

'You have to prepare yourself mentally for a proper dig like this. Wee Carl will know what I'm talking about', said Davy while injecting his left buttock with an anabolic steroid compound.

The 34-year-old described his own gruelling training regimen and strict diet which he's been adhering to:

'I get up about 11am and roll a fuck-off spliff. I take Sasha (his beloved German Shepherd) to the park for a run and a shite. Then it's straight down the gym for a bitta pad work'.

'I've had to switch from fried to boiled rice with my Salted Chilli Chicken from the Chinkers. And I've started drinking diet Coke with my forty ouncer of Vod. It's not been easy but these are the sacrifices the likes of myself and The Jackal have to make'.

And Davy's not the only one who can empathize with WBO interim featherweight Champion Frampton.

Thousands of men across the province are looking forward to getting hammered and saturating social media with their expert analysis of the fight.

34-year-old Barney Tumble, usually takes to Facebook to offer his opinion on where a fighter is going wrong, despite the fact his last physical confrontation with anyone took place at the sand pit in nursery school.

He said, 'As soon as I have a few beers and the fight is on, I start to play over in my head the brutal bout I took part in thirty years ago when little Jimmy Spence wrecked my sandcastle and then I pushed him'.

'I can totally put myself in Carl's shoes havin' won 23 of my 24 fair-digs in school', he added.

Rodney Roughhouse (27) is dreading watching the fight with his best mate Basher Stewart.

He told us, 'The only reason I'm going round there is because he has BT Sport'.

'It'll be interesting to see how many rounds will pass this time before he says 'this is what Frampton needs ta do in the next round'.

'Then he'll ask me 'Did ya see lat ler dig he hit yer mawn ler?' I feel like saying 'No every time it looks as though someone is about to land a punch I close my eyes – you dick'.

Winter Olympics moved to Dundonald amid security fears

The 23rd Winter Olympics has been moved to Dundonald Ice Bowl after the North Korean delegation in Pyeongchang turned out to be killer robots sent by evil leader Kim Jong Un.

Now the eyes of the world will be upon the sleepy County Down townland as it prepares to host its first ever Olympic games.

The East Belfast suburb fought off stern competition from Oslo, Calgary and Lisburn to secure the prestigious event.

Ballybeen had already attained Olympic Village status some time ago because of the large numbers of people in the area who wore tracksuits.

The games will take place at the International Ice Bowl and its surrounding car parks. The sports will include:

Skating-on-Speed;
Men's Horizontal Bar-Crawl
Freestyle-Fingering

- as well as the local past times of 'Shootin' and 'Baxin'.

The opening ceremony will start at 10am this morning in the car park and teams from far afield will parade proudly in front of the adoring crowds.

The Holywood flag bearer will be Farquhar Alcott, captain of the men's super-yacht racing team, whilst the Newtownards standard will be proudly carried by Rimpy Mayne, captain of the Men's 100m three-armed butterfly swimming team.

Dundonald built the Ice Bowl in 1986 with a view to hosting the 1992 Winter Olympics. Olympic committee officials visited the Ice Bowl in October '86 with Dundonald's bid reportedly leading the way ahead of Albertville and Lillehammer.

However it was during the ill-fated trip that a member of the Olympic delegation, Johan Burntbach, suffered second-degree burns on the Indianaland 'Free Fall' and the games went to Albertville instead.

Those athletes who make the podium will receive gold, silver and bronze sovereign rings.

IFA to replace national anthem with Maniac 2000

The Irish FA have announced they will replace the national anthem with classic floor-filler Maniac 2000 before Saturday's Irish Cup final between Coleraine and Cliftonville.

The move comes after the IFA's DJ received a written request from Cliftonville FC.

'I don't usually do requests', explained DJ Sammy C.

'But Cliftonville went to the effort of submitting it in writing on this lovely headed paper', he added.

Cliftonville's support predominantly comes from the commercial dance community and the north Belfast club are aiming to win the competition for the first time since 1979.

Famous supporter Tim McGarry welcomed the decision. He said: 'Fuck it's been a while since I heard that wee banger. The place will go nuts if they drop that before kick-off. I might see if I can get my hands on a few yokes'.

Maniac, released February 2000, was a Spide-Anthem played at every country club and hotel disco on loop for the better part of five years.

However, not everyone was welcomed the move with several clubs contacting the IFA to voice their disapproval.

Big Sandy Whiteside, chairman of the South Belfast Linfield Drinking Club, expressed his anger at the decision.

'The IFA are a disgrace. If they're gonna play an 'old skool' track, then it has to 'You're a Superstar' by Love Inc. Me and the boys threw a quare few shapes to thon back in the day, let me tell ye', he said.

Tonic wine flu to sweep Northern Ireland tonight

Experts fear a tonic wine-flu epidemic could be on its way to Northern Ireland.

The warning comes ahead of Northern Ireland's home fixture with the Czech Republic tonight at the National Stadium in Belfast.

Employers across the country are bracing themselves for an unprecedented level of absence tomorrow morning if a Tonic Wine-Flu outbreak does occur.

A stark warning in New Scientist said: 'The risk of the influenza to residents in Northern Ireland remains extremely high as Michael O'Neill's men stand on the brick of securing a World Cup play-off place'.

'Anyone intending to ingest large quantities of fortified Spide juice tonight is at great risk of contracting this deadly virus'.

'Those infected will experience symptoms which include: singing Neil Diamond songs; a compulsion to bounce up & down and a severe allergic reaction to attending work the next day'.

Block-booker Big Sandy Whiteside told us he wouldn't be surprised if he was struck down by the virus.

He said, 'That'd be just my luck. I get everything that's going about, so it wouldn't surprise me if I caught that aul' Tonic Wine-Flu the night'.

Meanwhile, Sandy's wife Sharon was having absolutely none of it. She said, 'He's a lying lazy big bastard so he is. No doubt he'll fall in here about 1am covered in kebab meat and smelling like a brewery'.

'Then he'll ring his boss in the morning, putting on his aul' sick voice, sounding like Marge Simpson with laryngitis'.

New Scientist claims there are some radical new treatments which may help anyone infected this evening.

'We would recommend administering large doses of milkman's orange and sausage meat wrapped in puff pastry to anyone contaminated by the virus', they said.

Man United fans always respected Europa League

A die-hard Manchester United fan has claimed that he always respected the integrity of the Europa League, it has emerged.

Kevin Gallagher, 43, made the announcement ahead of tonight's crucial game with Dutch side Ajax which could make or break United's season.

'I wasn't one of those people who used to call it a Mickey Mouse cup', said Kevin. 'Even when we were in the Champions League, I always considered it to be a major trophy'.

'In some ways it's actually better than winning the Champions League because you have to play more matches, therefore it's harder to win', he added.

When asked whether he used to taunt opposition supporters whose clubs participated in the competition during United's glory years, Gallagher said, 'Absolutely not. No way. Perish the thought'.

However, Kevin's brother, Jim, a Liverpool supporter, insists this may be a distorted version of the facts.

'F**king ballix', cried Jim. 'Every Thursday night he'd text me sayin' 'what's a Liverpool fan's favourite perfume?' 'Chanel No 5'.

'Every competition except for the Premier League and Champions League was Mickey f**kin' Mouse according to him', added Jim.

Liverpool man Jim has made his own preparations for tonight's showpiece game in Stockholm.

'I've changed my profile picture on Facebook to an Ajax badge', chuckled the 46-year-old father-of-three.

'I cannot wait until United lose', beamed Jim. 'That means all they have won this season is the League Cup'.

When we pointed out to Jim that the League Cup was only trophy Liverpool had won in the last ten seasons, spending £700m in the process, he rose to his feet and sang 'We won it five times, we won it five times…'.

Sports Day ruined by competitive wanker

A Dundonald man spoiled his son's first ever school sports day by taking it 'far too seriously', it has emerged.

Big Colin Bolt, 37, attended his 5-year-old son's inaugural sporting event hoping to exorcise the demons of his own failed athletics career which ended when he was thirteen.

Bolt spent the previous evening in the back garden stretching and slapping himself across the face to psyche himself up.

Then he drove to Decathlon at Holywood Exchange to buy a new pair of trainers in order to give himself the best possible chance of victory in the parent's race.

After exiting the shop, Bolt ingested an entire strip of Nandrolone pills and then felt a slight twinge in his left buttock.

He told us, 'It may well have been a fart but to be on the safe side, I instructed the wife to administer a painkilling injection directly into the arse-cheek'.

The following day when his son, Colin Jnr, lined up for the egg & spoon race, the 37-year-old stood on the side-lines heckling the other children.

The race was held up for several minutes when one child withdrew after claims that Bolt called him 'a fat wee dick with no neck'.

When the race finally resumed, little Colin Jnr made a great start, only to drop this egg a mere five metres from the finish line.

Despite recovering to secure a respectable 3rd place finish, whilst the rest of the children were being hugged by their parents, Colin Snr couldn't hide his disappointment and refused to make eye contact with his son.

Finally, the moment Colin Snr had been waiting for arrived and several adults lined up for the parent's race.

After several false starts triggered by an overeager Bolt, the race got underway. The 37-year-old made a great start and left the other disinterested overweight parents in his wake.

However, with the finish line in sight, the child that Bolt allegedly called 'a fat wee dick with no neck' stuck his foot out sending Colin Snr head over arse.

Bolt landed awkwardly, breaking his collar bone and dislocating his shoulder in the process.

When asked if he was upset that his father had broken his collar bone, Colin Jnr replied, 'Yes. I was hoping it was his neck'.

Ballymacash reveals new World Cup fan zone

Following the success of the Euro fanzones at Titanic Belfast, Ballymacash today unveiled their state of the art fanzone for this summer's World Cup.

The open air arena constructed at the site of the scenic Ballymacash bonfire will be showing all 64 games live and organisers have encouraged those who are free from the shackles of employment to come along and watch them all.

Games will be screened on a 50" Smart TV that lucky organisers found lying in the middle of the road after it had fallen off the back of lorry.

'Fuck all smart about it', said event co-ordinator 'Basher' Stewart. 'I've been asking it for my wife's credit card pin all morning and it hasn't even answered me'.

Fans can enjoy the games in style on one of the busted sofas strewn across the field or are invited bring along their own chairs, preferably wooden, which can then be burnt at a later date.

According to organisers the arena has full bar facilities, food options and entertainment before and after games.

'If ya run outta drink, the lads will be sellin' tins of green for a poun and Big 'Bap' McBride's ma will bring out the tamata & spawm samiches at half-time', beamed Basher.

'Before and after kick-off there'll be some under-15s bare-bellied amateur baxin' and a Sonic the Hedgehog bouncy castle for their kids', he added.

Community representative Cllr Joelene Hunter officially opened the arena by smashing a bottle of Prosecco off a stack of pallets.

'Ats us nai', she shouted amidst cries of 'yeeoo'.

Drunken Nacho Signs For DLA Galaxy.

Former Rangers player Nacho Novo ended up at a house party in Templemore Avenue and unwittingly signed a ten year contract with DLA Galaxy whilst heavily under the influence of Glens vodka, it has emerged

The Spanish forward has become increasingly embroiled in all things loyalist after hanging up the boots a few years ago. The diminutive striker was spotted mingling with locals on the Newtownards Road during yesterday's Twelfth of July celebrations.

Novo, 37, was dragged along to an after party by a group of males who couldn't believe their luck. Wee Willie 'Dinger' Bell, 22, coaxed the Spaniard back to a party with promises of 'sluts and gear all over le shap'. He told us, 'I said to ma mate, no way, lers yer mawn who played for Rangers'.

He added, 'None of the other c**ts back at the party wud believe until I put Novo on the phone and gat him to sing Penny Arcade'.

When he arrived at the party Novo was asked if he had any money for a K Kabs carry out. The youths then instructed Novo to 'keep dick' outside and wait on the taxi filled with alcohol.

It was whilst outside 'havin a feg' that Novo was approached by a young male who asked for his autograph. Unbeknownst to the Spaniard he was putting his signature towards a decade long legally binding contract to play for Dundonald 'bawd lot' DLA Galaxy.

Novo woke up about 8am this morning on a sofa using a tracksuit top as a blanket and when he searched for his phone he came across the contract.

He said, 'Does anyone know the number of a good taxi? And a better solicitor?'

Jackie Fullerton denies 'bucking' anyone's ma

Silver fox Jackie Fullerton has been forced to deny claims about his love life after Northern Ireland fans recently unfurled a banner that suggested the Ballymena man may have had sexual relations with your mother.

Fullerton has long enjoyed his status as one of Northern Ireland's biggest sex symbols, regularly pipping the likes of Daniel O'Donnell and Iain Dowie to the crown of 'Norn Iron's Biggest Ride' on numerous occasions.

In 2011 the permed lothario had to deny allegations made by the Sunday World that he had fathered close to 2,000 children. The story reported that Fullerton used his role of roaming Irish League commentator as a smoke-screen to lure nationwide fanny into his BBC trailer.

Despite the numerous claims made against him, the man with the half Ballymena – half John Wayne accent has always managed to emerge from the shite smelling like the roses he'd leave at the bedsides of a multitude of satisfied women.

However, as hordes of Northern Ireland fans look forward to a week's drinking in France armed with Buckfast and banners about Jackie, the former sports anchor is reportedly 'shitting a brick' about what revelations these flags might transmit across the globe.

The man whose immortal commentary sound bites include 'It's a goal – no it isn't' and 'Oh he's done it again. Jonny Evans scores his FIRST goal for Northern Ireland' told us, 'Well there you have it folks, they're saying that I 'bucked your ma-a'. I haven't been this embarrassed since I tried the German pronunciation of Austria and told everyone at home that we were drawing 1-1 with a large flightless bird'.

One woman, who didn't wish to be named, told our reporters that she was a mother and Jackie had indeed bucked her on several occasions. She told us, 'I remember how he'd bring a copy of the team sheet into bed the night before a big game. The more difficult the names were to pronounce, the more aroused he became'.

She continued, 'I remember Northern Ireland played Iceland back in 2006. You should've heard him trying to say Kristjan Finnbogason. Big Jackie was shooting before he got anywhere near the box'.

ABOUT THE AUTHOR

The Dundonald Liberation Army is the brainchild of Northern Irish writer Stephen G. Large. The 37-year-old's debut self-published title 'A Concise History of the Dundonald Liberation Army' stormed to the top of Amazon Kindle Download Charts within a week of its release in March of 2016. His second title, A Dog DLA Afternoon peaked at #6 in the Kindle Comedy/Parody Charts during the first month of its release in May 2017. Stephen has written for television, stage and radio whilst his online content for the BBC has so far received over 25 million views.

Printed in Great Britain
by Amazon